WHEN DR. GRUMPY MET HER SUNSHINE

AMY BLYTHE

MEDICAL ROMANCE

Recycling programs for this product may not exist in your area.

ISBN-13: 978-1-335-99382-3

When Dr. Grumpy Met Her Sunshine

For questions and comments about the quality of this book, please contact us at CustomerService@Harlequin.com.

Harlequin Enterprises ULC
22 Adelaide St. West, 41st Floor
Toronto, Ontario M5H 4E3, Canada
www.Harlequin.com

HarperCollins Publishers
Macken House, 39/40 Mayor Street Upper,
Dublin 1, D01 C9W8, Ireland
www.HarperCollins.com

Printed in U.S.A.

1 2 3 4 5 6 7 8 9 10 HDC 28 27 26 25

He cleared his throat. “I could be a little jealous.” He held her gaze. “The nurses think you’re seeing Dr. Pierce.”

“What?”

“So we’re probably safe a while yet.”

“I don’t love that they’re speculating about me at all.”

“It’s all the smiling.”

“What? Do I not normally smile?” She gave a sigh, head spinning. Was she really that much of a grump the rest of the time that a good mood was so notable? “My whole career I’m told to work on my bedside manner, be more friendly, and now it’s gonna bite me in the arse. Didn’t anyone notice you’re looking pretty smug and sated?” But as soon as she asked the question, she knew the answer. “I guess you’re always so positive and friendly and warm—the contrast is more pronounced because I’m usually such a grump.”

He laughed. “I like your grumpy face.”

“Shut up.” She reached for the door, ready to walk out.

He put out an arm to stop her. It was at hip height, so she walked straight into it, enjoying the touch, however brief it must be.

Dear Reader,

Wouldn't it be nice if things were simpler? Reading can be a wonderful, much-needed escape from all the complexity of real life. I'm excited for Cam and Sasha's story to whisk you away on a romantic getaway. But in some ways, this book is very real. Cam and his sister's relationship is based on my own siblings: how we help (ahem, interfere) in one another's lives, wind each other up and teach one another things. Sasha's experience—coming home after living overseas, feeling isolated and misunderstood but also empowered by all she's learned in the big, wide world—that's what it was like for me! And then there are the inequities so ingrained in health care systems, which both Cam and Sasha grapple with.

But romance is the genre of hope. The happily-ever-after is guaranteed, so there's always hope, no matter how dark, twisty and *real* things get. As Emily Dickinson wrote, "Hope is the thing with feathers that perches in the soul, and sings the tune without the words, and never stops at all."

May Cam and Sasha's story give you a delightful escape and, if you need it, a spark of hope.

xx

Amy

Amy Blythe (she/her) is a hopeless romantic. She cannot get enough of that whooshing feeling you get from a significant look, a hand flex, a world-spinning kiss or an accidental mid-argument confession of love. She lives in Ōtautahi Christchurch with her husband, two teenagers and one enormous, fluffy cat (to whom she is allergic). A high school English teacher by day, she also runs an interschool poetry slam despite never memorizing anything longer than a haiku. The first novel she wrote was Jane Austen fan fiction, the second, ER fan fiction. And that probably tells you everything you need to know.

Books by Amy Blythe

Harlequin Medical Romance

Emergency Room Reunion

Visit the Author Profile page at Harlequin.com.

To Hannah and Ian—thanks for all the joy (and low-key torture) of a childhood spent inventing imaginary worlds, winding each other up for sport and rewatching the same six VHS tapes (*Three Men and a Little Lady*, *Sister Act 2*, a few random *Friends* episodes, *Little Women*, *Independence Day* and *Notting Hill*) till we could quote them all, beginning to end. Pivot!

CHAPTER ONE

SASHA MCBRIDE HAD a healthy relationship with risk. A fair few spine reconstructions, innumerable joint replacements, bone grafts, amputations and everything in between—in surgery, she juggled the known and unknown. But standing at the bus stop that morning, she was glad her teenage niece, Mya, had sent her off with instructions. Where was the high-flier superstar surgeon who'd left Chicago not even a month ago? What was it about moving home that could knock all of the confidence out of a person? How could lil' old Christchurch, New Zealand, make a renowned orthopaedic specialist feel like a child?

She scanned the QR code beside the bus map, just as Mya had told her to. Twelve minutes till the next bus. Three times longer than she was used to waiting for public transport.

She was a long way from Chicago now. Moving home was a real mixed bag. On the upside, she had family here, the weather was better; life was in many ways safer, easier, healthier. She was glad to be back, but it had been a long time—it was a shock to the system, for sure.

Eleven minutes. She could listen to a podcast while she waited.

No, she was too nervous to pay attention. Silly, really, because it wasn't even her first day—she'd been in and out all week with orientation and meetings, all the hospital on-boarding stuff that was supposed to ensure she was ready for today. Time to hit the ground running.

Her gaze fell on the bus route map, the oddly familiar grid of city streets. Her mind supplied memories from concerts in that park over there, to shopping with her friends on that street there, to discovering underground bars in those alleys there.

A lot of those places didn't exist any more. Between earthquakes and time passing, the Christchurch she knew had changed irrevocably. And so had she.

Nine minutes.

'How long does it say?' A guy in a wheelchair slowed to a stop beside her.

'Oh, nine—no, eight minutes.'

'Sweet. I thought I'd missed it.' He gave a relieved laugh and dropped his shoulders, visibly relaxing. It was a great laugh, and those were some great shoulders. He flicked on his brakes and pulled a satchel bag around onto his lap. She was staring at his arms—why was she staring at a complete stranger's arms?

And he clearly noticed.

'Sorry,' she said. 'Aren't you cold?' As if she were ogling those biceps out of concern for his catching a chill.

But he shrugged as though he bought the line. 'I run hot. And they've got the heaters on in the buses already.'

It was mid-March, early autumn. Sasha had her grey woollen coat open, a soft scarf loose around her neck. Whereas her bus-stop companion wore a short-sleeved, deep blue polo shirt. The unbuttoned collar exposed a few curls of chest hair—that was the moment she realised she was staring again.

Six minutes. Maybe a podcast was a good idea.

Cam McColl pulled his Metrocard from his wallet. The blonde-haired beauty at the bus stop was putting her earbuds in.

'The unauthorised release of beavers into British waterways,' said a male voice with an English accent, 'is known as beaver bombing.' It was coming from her phone.

Cam laughed.

The woman then realised, obviously, that her Bluetooth had not in fact connected, and fumbled her phone in a rush to pause it. English podcaster went on: 'So the River Otter is now full of beavers.'

She found the pause button and pulled out the earbud. 'These things are so temperamental. Oh, bus.' She put her arm out and waved way more than necessary. No wedding ring, Cam noticed. He couldn't help himself. For the first time in his adult life, he was living alone. A whole house to himself. Dating no longer involved carefully timed entrances and exits to avoid his mum. She was a great mum, very supportive, mostly open-minded, and happy to see him happy, but just the idea she might overhear something…shudder.

The bus driver put the ramp down, and the podcast woman stepped back to let Cam board. She was undeniably gorgeous: plump, pink-flushed cheeks and an expressive mouth, sharp eyes and spun-sunlight hair, but if she tried to push his wheelchair, or assumed he needed help…always a quick mood killer.

She didn't, though. She picked up the ramp behind him and didn't apologise when the driver told her she wasn't supposed to do that. 'I'll know for next time,' she said.

Cam backed his chair into the wheelchair spot, reaching for the belt—he did this so often, he was on autopilot, which meant he didn't miss a beat of Podcast Woman trying to pay her bus fare with a credit card.

'We take cash or Metrocard,' the driver said. 'The new payment system isn't up and running yet.'

'I don't think I have…' She was digging in her purse.

'Here,' Cam said, and held out his card. 'Use mine.'

'I might have some cash.'

There was no way this woman in her sleek coat and understated gold jewellery was carrying cash.

She was all class and curves, head to toe. No flashy sneakers or bling, and she was riding the bus, so clearly she had nothing to prove, meaning she was likely loaded.

Out of his league? Absolutely. But she took his bus card and thanked him profusely.

As the bus pulled out into traffic, she sat opposite him. 'My niece told me where the stop was, and which side of the road, and how much it cost and how to check the schedule.' She gave a breathy laugh. 'Failed to mention I'd need cash. I can pay you back.'

'Don't worry about it. When did you last take the bus?'

'In Christchurch? Um…' She was clearly counting back a long time in her head, a cute quizzical look on her face. 'I was a teenager. Enough said.'

'What, five or six years ago?'

'Hah!' The laugh leapt out of her, then she seemed to forcibly turn serious. 'Anyway, thanks for paying my fare. Wouldn't be a good look, late to work on my first week.'

'You can get a Metrocard at the bus exchange.'

'Right. Thanks.'

'Cam.'

'Huh?'

'My name is Cam.'

'Oh, thanks, Cam,' she said, but didn't offer her own name. Okay, so he was striking out here. Not gonna happen.

He pulled out his own headphones, silently letting her off the conversational hook. She put in her earbuds a moment later and this time didn't broadcast her podcast to everyone nearby. Which left him slightly disappointed—would he ever find out what beaver bombing was all about?

Cam listened to his morning hype-up playlist while he read over his client's notes. Joshua Tait, fifty-seven, was two months post-operative, a lower-limb amputee due to diabetes. A high school teacher, basketball coach and church elder, he'd even done a stint on the local city council. Clearly a proactive, community-minded guy. Cam knew better than to make assumptions, but this man's recovery would likely go one of two ways: he'd want to get back into everything as if he didn't have a brand-new disability to contend with—classic denial, with a chaser of immense frustration—or he'd be feeling completely useless, stuck, unable to do anything he used to love and possibly on the path to depression.

The bus was pulling into the station. Podcast Woman stood up, gave him a smile of acknowledgement and moved towards the door. But she wasn't ready for the speed bumps and, grabbing at the railing, landed directly in his lap. 'Oh, God, I'm so sorry,' she said, trying to stand up.

And then the second speed bump brought her grinding back into him.

He laughed. 'Maybe just stay put until it stops.' Between her coat and scarf, the shape of her body had been fairly well hidden, but he was very aware of it now.

She stood up, two hands on the railing, clearly determined not to ride him the rest of the way in. 'If I fall on my face now, it won't even be the most embarrassing thing I've done today.'

'Speaking as someone who's done some top-tier face plants, I wouldn't recommend it.'

Her eyes went wide.

'Landing on another person is definitely your best-case scenario.'

'Only injuring my pride.'

'Eh, who needs it?'

The bus came to a stop and she didn't immediately let go of the railing. Cam unbuckled himself from the wall. 'Go ahead.' He gestured to the exit, and off she went, her long coat flapping behind her, the electric light in the depot making her blonde hair almost glow. If this were a movie, she'd turn around and look back at him. But this was real life.

Waiting for the ramp, he had a strange feeling he'd remember this moment. That he'd be looking for her every time he got on the bus for weeks to come. A tad pathetic? Yes. Still, it was the best bus ride into work in a long time.

Sasha walked away, the cool morning air like a caress against her blush-warm cheeks. If she had to humiliate herself in public, why did it have to be in front of someone—in fact, *on top* of someone—with such a brilliant smile and quick sense of humour? And there was something about those sea-green eyes, as though he noticed every little detail about her, saw her most minute reactions. Possibly even read her mind.

Okay, he also had nice arms. Very nice arms.

Was riding the bus magically transporting her back in time? Embarrassed and awkward like a teenager because a cute guy talked to her, maybe even flirted a little.

Sasha slowed her step. She'd basically run away the moment the bus stopped. The sense of a missed opportunity landed on her shoulders, a twinge of regret. She checked the time—she was early. She could get herself that Metrocard. A perfectly valid excuse to return to the bus station.

Sasha joined the short queue at the information kiosk and kept her gaze fixed to the signage on the walls—posters promising new payment options 'coming soon' in amongst more useful information for someone new in town, but shamelessly looking for the guy from the bus was the only other option and—oh, this was ridiculous! She gave in, glanced around. No sign of him. Probably for the best.

Brand-new Metrocard in hand, she walked out of the bus station towards the hospital. It wasn't her first day back, so she shouldn't be surprised by how unfamiliar the city looked—how much it had changed while she'd been off studying and then working, and then studying some more, and working some more. It wasn't just the architecture that had changed, but the people, too: most of her friends had left, or she'd simply lost touch. In many ways, moving to Christchurch was less like coming home and more like starting over some place new.

As she walked alongside the river, there was one thing that hadn't changed: the old oak and chestnut trees with their leaves turning orange and red were lining the pavement, clogging up the gutters, yet above her head, the ruddy foliage made the blue sky look too bright to be real.

It almost made up for the otherwise humiliating start to her day—beaver bombing? The timing was brutal, and relying on a stranger to pay her bus fare wasn't ideal, but falling in his lap… If she could pull a muscle from cringing, she'd be limping right now.

At the last crossing before the hospital, someone in a wheelchair was waiting for the lights. His arms gave him away. And his hair—warm caramel brown, wavy and tidy, but easy to imagine all mussed and chaotic—and what the hell was wrong with her? Was she so starved for touch that falling in his lap had flicked the switch? She'd broken up with Liam only a few weeks ago. She was too smart for a rebound. No point pretending this was anything other than hormones and coincidences.

But he was heading towards the hospital. Was he a patient? God, if he was *her* patient, that would be bad.

But she shouldn't assume, because he used a wheelchair, that he wasn't entirely healthy. He might be visiting someone. Clearly he was a nice guy, kind to strangers with no bus fare. If she was going to completely embarrass herself, it had to be in front of one of the good ones.

She slowed her pace, hoping not to catch up to him. He swung left to take the ramp up the final rise. Sasha turned right and took the stairs. Orthopaedics was on the fourth floor. At the elevators, she thumbed the close button as if her life depended on it.

Now she'd probably wonder all day—all week—if he was roaming the halls of the same building, expect to see him around every corner, in every elevator and waiting room.

He was not, however, visiting any of her patients on rounds. Nor was he behind the computer, retrieving her updated schedule. Sasha needed to keep her head in the game—not that the work was especially challenging compared with Northwestern, but she was new, and she did have a tendency to be a little abrupt sometimes. Blunt, Liam would say. Rude was what he meant. Sasha liked to think of herself as direct and honest and devoid of bullshit. She didn't always make a great first impression. Long story short, she needed to focus on her work, on getting the little things right, and not letting some guy she met on the bus distract her. But she could have sworn she glimpsed his hair through one of the internal windows, though the height was off for someone in a wheelchair. She turned around and found herself face to face with her new boss. 'Dr Stirling,' Sasha said.

'Call me Vivian,' said Dr Stirling.

Sasha nodded, but couldn't quite bring herself to do it. The woman was too impressive for one little name. She was one of those people who seemed taller than they really were.

'We were interrupted on Tuesday,' continued Dr Stirling—Vivian.

'I've read through the rest of the orientation materials, and everyone's been really helpful.'

'*Kei te pai*,' she said in Māori. *That's good.* Sasha recognised the phrase—snippets of the indigenous language were commonly interwoven with English here, but Sasha was rusty. Maybe she should add a language-learning podcast to her playlist.

'I have got a few questions,' Sasha said. 'But I have a post-op appointment now.'

Dr Stirling smiled. 'Find me afterwards?'

'Will do. Where is 2 Ox?'

'That's Outpatients.'

'Yes, but where in the hospital?'

'You haven't been over the road?' Vivian checked her watch. 'I can walk with you now.'

Sasha was almost jogging to keep up as her boss strode ahead to the elevators.

'Full schedule today?' Dr Stirling asked.

'I have follow-ups this morning—a lower-limb amputee and then two hip replacements and a knee.'

'Then surgery this afternoon?'

'Arthroscopic rotator cuff. Two of them, back-to-back.'

'I was going to ask if you wanted to come along

tonight—there's a fundraiser thing, but I totally understand if you'll be wiped out after all that.'

'Fundraiser thing?' Sasha said, and heard the undisguised scepticism in her own voice. In Chicago, once she'd moved up the ranks, there'd been an expectation, and she'd gone along to many such events. But she was no good at schmoozing, at turning on the charm, at pretending she didn't fundamentally object to a medical system that relied on begging for scraps from philanthropists more interested in stroking their egos than actually helping people.

'I know,' Vivian said, as if she felt exactly the same way. 'I don't know how I got myself into this—being auctioned off for charity.'

'What's the cause?' Sasha asked.

'Kidney Foundation. I shouldn't complain—I'm giving up an evening, not a kidney.'

Sasha couldn't help but admire Vivian's attitude. 'Maybe I should bid on you, save you from some skeevy old man.'

'I've already organised a friend to do just that.'

Sasha was off the hook, then. She should have felt relieved. Instead she felt… FOMO. Was this envy or just good old-fashioned loneliness? Vivian had friends, people she could call on. Of course she did. She didn't need Sasha. But Vivian was the closest thing Sasha had to a friend here. And Vivian was her boss, so that was officially pathetic.

'Other than the bit when I get up on stage and

find out my dollar value—' Vivian grimaced '—it should be a fun night.'

It'd be hell, but Sasha could do with making some friends. Making a good impression wouldn't hurt either. She knew how she came across. 'Maybe it would be good to…' She was about to say *make a good impression* but that was probably a bit too transparent. 'To get to know people.'

'Yeah, that's what I thought.' Vivian led the way outside. At a buzz, she checked her watch. She looked worried.

'Everything okay?'

'I need to go scrub in. You're headed to that building with the orange girders. Ask at the desk and someone will point you in the right direction.'

'Thanks.'

'One of these days we'll get through a full conversation uninterrupted.'

'I wouldn't bet on it,' Sasha said, the words just slipping out as if she were chatting to an old friend, not her new boss.

But Vivian Stirling smiled. 'This evening, perhaps.'

CHAPTER TWO

CAM'S PHONE BUZZED for the fourth time in two minutes.

'You should get that,' his patient said. 'I really don't mind.' The man was far too accommodating. Navigating the medical system with a disability, in Cam's vast experience, went better for those who were unapologetically demanding. Proverbial squeaky wheels.

'I'll just put it on "do not disturb",' Cam said, but while he did that he saw he had three texts and a missed call from his sister. It was probably a childcare crisis. Her kid was thirteen and more than capable of staying alive for a couple of hours unsupervised.

'Everything okay?' Joshua said.

'Yeah, absolutely. Which doctor did they say you had?'

'McBride. Do you know them?'

'The name doesn't ring a bell, but don't worry. You'll get your wound checked, answer a bunch of questions, and then you'll ask your questions, say what you need. I'll mostly just listen and take some notes, but if you feel like you're not being heard or the doctor's not being clear, I can jump in.'

Joshua nodded.

Cam saw her a fraction of a second before she spoke—Podcast Woman. 'Joshua Tait?' She looked up from a clipboard. Then she saw Cam and her cheeks went bright pink.

'That's me.' Joshua wheeled his chair forward.

Cam couldn't move his arms.

'I'm Dr McBride. Sasha.' She put out her hand and Joshua shook it, then she turned to Cam.

'Sorry, brake issue.' Cam pretended to fix an imaginary glitch with his wheelchair, which, if real, could actually be serious, but desperate times. 'I'm with Disability Advocacy Services,' Cam said. 'I'm Mr Tait's support person.' Never mind that he'd met Joshua Tait an hour ago; it was better if doctors believed he'd been with his patients through thick and thin—better they didn't doubt where his loyalties lay.

'This is Cam,' Joshua said.

Cam had forgotten that bit. Because he'd already introduced himself to her. And then she'd pointedly *not* given her name, despite briefly sitting in his lap…

'Nice to meet you both,' she said, the blush gone from her cheeks already. 'We're just down the hall here.' She turned and she wasn't wearing the long woollen coat any more. Nothing but his own meagre willpower to keep him from watching her hips sway—and right in his eyeline, too. But what was the alternative? Driving his chair with his eyes closed?

'We're in here,' she said, and held the door open, and pointedly did *not* make eye contact with Cam. Probably because she thought she'd embarrassed herself. And his not-so-subtle enjoyment of…well, everything about their encounter probably made it worse.

Sasha McBride. The name suited her—the fresh sibilance of Sasha, with the blonde hair and the bright eyes and soft curves, followed by the serious surname, old-fashioned, a bit grumpy and Scottish, a bit romantic. Dr McBride.

'How's your recovery going, Mr Tait?' she asked.

Joshua shrugged. 'All right.'

'Two months since the surgery?' she asked, then went over all the clinical details, clearly and precisely, without dumbing it down or hiding behind jargon. Cam was impressed. Joshua was visibly relaxing long before she checked his wound. 'Any irritation or pain?'

'I still get an itch on my…well, where my foot was.'

'How often is that?' There was something about her tone, the interest in her eyes, that coaxed the man into an honest admission of all his discomforts and challenges. She made it look easy, and Cam knew better—he'd had a full hour with Joshua and spent a good portion of it convincing the guy that being honest about his experiences wasn't *complaining*.

'Phantom pain isn't something to shrug off,' Sasha said, carefully trimming some wound tape. 'There's really only one proven treatment—targeted muscle reinnervation. I'd recommend talking to a plastic surgeon.'

'I don't really care about how it looks,' Mr Tait said.

She walked around Cam's chair, pointing to a poster—a diagram of the human body. 'All these nerves—' she traced the blue and red lines down the leg to the ankle '—they need somewhere to go and something to do. We can't just switch them off. But we can redirect them.'

'You mean another surgery?'

'It's the only thing that consistently works for phantom pain.'

'I really don't want another surgery.'

She gave a nod, and looked as if she was biting back words.

'I read about a nerve-blocker and some kind of mirror therapy.'

'Anecdotally, these things have helped *some* patients. Nerve-blockers can be effective, but there are side effects as with any medication. I couldn't make any promises.'

It was rare to hear a doctor so unequivocal and absolute. Cam couldn't decide if he liked the directness, the certainty. There was an arrogance to it. She was clearly uninterested in espousing the details of those unproven alternatives.

'Will the phantom pain be worse if I get a…you know, a prosthetic?'

'Shouldn't be, but nerves can be tricky.'

Joshua nodded.

'You can put your leg down now,' she said, and took off her gloves.

Joshua rearranged himself in his chair. 'So what else can I try?'

'Targeted muscle reinnervation would be my recommendation—it'll also improve the fitting of your prosthesis. With minimal discomfort, you'll regain a lot of mobility.'

This was Cam's cue. 'Targeted muscle reinnervation is a surgery, though.'

She nodded. 'But it's far less invasive than what you've been through. The recovery is significantly simpler. And the benefits are enormous.'

'I can't take a whole lot more time off work,' Joshua said.

Again, she looked as if she was biting back her response, but Cam could imagine what she thought. This was why he was here. 'I think we're keen to look at the non-surgical options.'

She met his gaze and seemed to deflate. 'I can refer you to a cognitive therapist. And we can start on a low dose of nortriptyline. Do you already have a physio you like?'

They parted ways a few minutes later with a prescription and an alarming list of possible side effects. Cam saw Joshua off and parked his chair outside in the sunshine. He had seven texts from his sister.

Want to come to a fancy party tonight? My treat.

Sorin swapped shifts so I'm going solo. (Sad face emoji.)

There will be lots of women.

It's for charity.

Call me when you get a minute.

It's fundraising for kidney disease. (Heart emoji. Blood droplets emoji. Prayer hands.)

Good Lord, Neroli.

Did I mention all the (rich) women? (Fire emoji.)

He hit call, but it went straight to voicemail. She was probably working, just there, over the road beyond two ambulances and the big Emergency sign.

'Oh, good, you're still here.' Sasha strode out of the outpatient building, straight towards him. 'I was hoping to catch you.'

'Dr McBride,' he said, plastering on a smile.

'I just wanted to give you this.' She handed over an envelope. 'Some information, that's all.'

'About the surgery he's not interested in having.'

'I worked with the doctor who developed this

technique in Chicago. It really is worth considering—the success rate is astronomical, and I understand further surgery is daunting but…'

'But he was pretty clear he didn't want it.'

'People change their minds. Chronic pain is no picnic.'

'No kidding,' Cam said.

She seemed to notice then that he was in a wheelchair, which was strangely refreshing—most people saw the chair before the person. But then she was a doctor. A surgeon, no less. The bar should be higher for someone like that, at the top of their field.

Cam took the envelope. 'I'll take a read.'

'That's all I'm asking. The other options he mentioned are honestly a waste of time and resources. Every scrap of evidence is entirely anecdotal.'

He pivoted his chair to face her. 'That only means there's no funding for proper research.'

She was clearly caught by surprise at his understanding of the system, but she didn't argue, only gave a cold nod of acknowledgement. Then she said, 'His physio is going to give him a long list of exercises and just enough hope that, when it doesn't work, the disappointment will be crushing.'

'Not a high chance he's feeling much hope right now,' he said, and felt a twinge of regret, because it wouldn't do anyone any good for him to make an enemy of a surgeon. He should know better. How many times had he played nice with much worse than Sasha McBride? It was the only way to get the job done: catch more flies with honey.

But rather than mend his fences he took his out: the crossing went green and he wheeled away from her as fast as his calloused hands could carry him.

Sasha marched back to her office and reopened the file on Mr Tait. She wasn't in the wrong here, but she would be damned sure the man had a good physio. Of course she didn't recognise any of the names, but she could ask around. Maybe a hospital physio would be more inclined to support a surgical option. Less likely to book him in every other week for the foreseeable future, making a small fortune off the guy for the sake of a bit of muscle tone and no real pain relief.

The hospital staff directory served up photos and contact information for all the hospital physios. Her picture was probably in here somewhere—oh, God, was it the same as the one on her ID badge? Worse than a passport photo. So she was busy freaking out about the bags under her eyes when she landed on the photo of Cameron McColl. Physiotherapist.

Cam was a physio.

What had she said—had she perhaps insulted his entire profession? Why hadn't he told her he was a physio? He'd let her run her mouth, bemoaning long lists of exercises and something about giving just enough hope to crush their patients when it failed.

And those sharp eyes of his, that quick sense of humour—the guy was clearly smart, he paid attention, and he hadn't missed a beat. She'd implied physios were a waste of time, and he'd heard exactly that.

He could have just said, *oh, by the way, I'm a physio.* He probably wasn't trying to bring her down a notch. She was the one putting her foot in her mouth. He was simply…letting her.

In that moment, she almost wished she could lump him in with the innumerable male egos she'd battled with since graduating medical school—since starting medical school, come to think of it. But Cam McColl didn't seem the type to take issue with being outranked by a woman.

The thought itself made her groan. She hated all that hierarchical, power-tripping nonsense. She didn't really believe in the ranking system that would place a surgeon higher than any other practitioner, but enough people did that it had a real impact on the way things worked.

That's just the way things are, Liam's voice rang in her ears like a gong. A frustrating, disappointing, infuriating, reverberating, headache-inducing gong. *Either play the game or get off the court.* The relationship had finally ended when she left Chicago, and she wasn't missing his voice in her ear. Wasn't missing anything about him, in fact. Working and living with him, she'd been desperate to get away long before she'd actually left.

Liam had a talent for sounding logical, irrefutable, even when he was saying things she outright disagreed with. Made her feel crazy. Well, at the end she'd felt crazy. At the beginning, she'd felt chosen, privy to the honest opinions of someone who wasn't easy to impress. She'd thought his critical mind and sharp tongue would make her better, stronger—that she would always be improving if she could only toughen up and take the 'constructive feedback'. Instead she'd shrunk to fit the mould, attempting to soften all her rough edges, and it had never been enough. Going against her own moral code—that was what it had felt like. Dishonest and fake. Exhausting.

But she was free now. Except she hadn't quite shaken off his hold on her mind.

That's just the way things are, Liam would say. *I thought you valued honesty.* The way he messed with her head… She should have got out much sooner.

Ugh. *That's just the way things are.* Was that how she'd sounded, talking to Mr Tait? Talking to Cam? *That's just the way things are.* She hadn't meant to be so dismissive, but good intentions didn't count for much.

A notification bleeped at her from the computer and for a moment she thought it might be Cam, back for round two, but no, it was only an email. An invitation. The Kidney Foundation fundraiser.

CHAPTER THREE

SASHA WAS QUITE possibly dreaming. This was one of those lucid nightmares where you thought you'd woken up but you were still in it. What other possible explanation was there for her current situation—on stage, in her slinkiest dress, in front of a couple of hundred strangers and her boss?

She could blame her boss, at least partially. But the real reason Sasha had let herself be talked into this was probably deeper. Something about being new and wanting to be seen as a good sport—something to counterbalance the less-than-perfect first impression she had a tendency to make. Imposter syndrome might be part of it, but atoning for what had happened with Mr Tait this afternoon certainly was not.

Volunteering for this charity auction, this farce, had nothing at all to do with Cam McColl, disability advocate and undercover physio. They'd cross paths on the ward and maybe he'd sit alongside some of her outpatients appointments in his advocacy role, but they wouldn't be working closely together. He wasn't scrubbing in on surgery, and she didn't have time for small talk with her post-ops.

The art gallery was made up of towering glass panels reflecting the whole party, all the other surgeons, their partners, the hospital executives, a few politicians and others who would benefit from being seen at a philanthropic event. Sasha hoped only to be seen as she was: hard working and reliable. A team player. Earning a little social credit was a good idea given that her tendency towards blunt honesty did sometimes burn through her colleagues' goodwill. Other than Liam, no one had ever called her difficult to her face, but she'd lost count of how many times she'd been warned not to be *seen* as difficult. Usually by a head of department or some higher-up. Often while they were in the process of promoting her. She'd done well professionally—didn't have anything to prove there—but she hadn't made a lot of friends.

She'd wanted a clean slate when she moved home, and she had a bad feeling she'd smudged it already.

So here she was, about to be auctioned off for charity. It was too surreal. But Vivian Stirling had opened the bidding, so maybe this wouldn't end in some awkward not-really-a-date with a complete stranger who thought he'd bought more than dinner and conversation.

The auctioneer was talking her up: 'Dr McBride comes to us from Northwestern in Chicago. A celebrated orthopaedic surgeon, she's fresh off the plane, and bound to have all sorts of fascinating stories—should make for sparkling dinner conversation.' No pressure, then.

Someone raised the bid. Then Vivian raised her hand again. Oh, thank goodness. She wasn't going to let Sasha be sold off to some random.

Next another woman bid—was that Vivian's friend?

Another stranger bid. Then another. Sasha's price wasn't getting anything near Vivian's two grand, but a respectable almost half that. Someone else at Vivian's table put their hand up—someone vaguely familiar.

'Sold!'

Vivian stood up, clapping and beckoning Sasha over to their table.

'What a good sport,' the auctioneer was saying. 'Welcome to Christchurch, Dr McBride!'

It had been a strange day, truly bizarre from start to finish, and it wasn't over yet. There beside Vivian's friend was Cam. She'd just been purchased at auction by Cam McColl.

'Hi,' Sasha said, not sure if she should sit or stand. Cam's face was impossible to read—amusement, surprise, uncertainty, maybe regret—all tucked behind a smile. But now was no time to stare at his mouth or attempt to read his mind.

Vivian stepped forward to make the introductions. 'This is Neroli, she works in ED, so we have her to thank for all our trauma patients.'

'Hey, I'm just the middleman. Middle-woman. Don't blame the middle-woman.' Clearly a couple of glasses of the bubbly had already been consumed. Neroli came around to shake hands and then pulled out a chair for Sasha. 'You've already met my brother, Cam.'

Oh, God, had he already told Sasha's colleagues the whole humiliating bus saga or, worse, discussed her treatment of Mr Tait?

Neroli held up a bottle of prosecco.

'Yes, please.' Sasha had definitely earned one of those. She could see Cam in her periphery, could feel his gaze on her. What was that look? Why had he bid on her? She didn't have the best emotional barometer, but she'd assumed he didn't like her much. 'Thanks for, ah, buying me?'

He cracked a smile. 'It's just a date. For a good cause.'

Right, of course. He was a good guy, doing a nice thing, and she shouldn't read more into it than that. But of all the people he could have bid on this evening…

The next auction began—a man this time. Neroli turned to Vivian. 'Isn't he married?'

'Maybe his wife will buy him.'

Several hands went up as the bidding began. Vivian and Neroli's conversation continued out of Sasha's earshot in the hubbub, leaving her and Cam to keep each other company.

She caught his eye—he seemed to think it was funny, bumping into each other for the third time in one day. 'You didn't mention you're a physiotherapist,' she said.

'You looked me up?'

'Not on purpose.'

He grinned, his face lighting up with laugh lines and dimples. 'If you say so, Dr McBride.'

'I was looking for Mr Tait's physio.'

'He's already on the service, so no need to refer him.' He cocked his head to the side and looked at her as if he'd puzzle out the mystery one way or another.

'Yes, well, as our auctioneer just pointed out, I'm new. Still getting my bearings. I wanted to be thorough.'

'Lucky Mr Tait.'

She couldn't tell if he was being sarcastic.

'We'll probably cross paths pretty often,' he said. 'I work on your ward.'

'Ah.'

'Not to mention we share a bus route.'

'Oh, I'm just staying with my sister for a couple of weeks until I find a place of my own. Not that I want to avoid you.' His forehead crinkled at that. She was putting her foot in her mouth again, and she couldn't even blame the bubbly; she'd only had two sips. 'After today, I wouldn't be surprised if you were the one avoiding me.'

He gave a one-shouldered shrug, drawing her attention to his shoulders, which felt a little unfair—he filled out that suit just right. 'I'm not that easily put off,' he said.

Neroli leaned over and beckoned him close, whispering not especially quietly, 'She's gorgeous, and Vivian says she's borderline genius.'

He moved the prosecco bottle out of easy reach and turned back to Sasha. 'So, staying with your sister. Does she drive you up the wall?'

It was like a magic trick. How did he do that? Laugh off embarrassment and make everyone feel better? Sasha had been all prickly and defensive mere seconds ago and now…now she was openly discussing her relationship with her sister. 'We get on all right. We've lived oceans apart our whole adult lives, so we're not super close.'

'Can't relate.' He threw a melodramatic but good-humoured glare at his sister.

'She's got a lot on her plate, but she's good value.' Truth was, Sasha had hardly seen her sister, between their different work schedules.

'And when you were younger?'

'She did let me borrow her ID card when I was underage.'

He laughed, and it felt far too good to earn it. He lifted his glass of bubbles.

'To sisters?' Sasha said.

'To the women who weren't supposed to raise us, and if they could just stop now that'd be great.'

'She did teach me to walk in heels.' Sasha had no idea why she was telling him so much. Every word that slipped out of her mouth surprised her.

'Neroli taught me to walk, period.'

Sasha felt her face react to that—her surprise,

confusion and curiosity turned up to full volume even though she hadn't said a word.

'I'm just messing with you,' Cam said.

'You can w—? Sorry, none of my business.'

He stood up then, reaching across the table for the bread basket.

Sasha noticed several things in quick succession: he was taller than she'd imagined, and apparently she had imagined; also, his butt was right in her face and she didn't mind at all; lastly, his shirt was rucked up, and she was way too tempted to reach out and trace the subtle ridge of abdominal muscle…

He sat back down. 'Did I shake it?' He'd caught her looking! He was asking if he'd shaken his rear.

She was probably blushing, definitely smiling. Avoiding his eyes, she watched his hands tear open a dinner roll.

'I do shake a fair bit,' he said, closer to serious now. 'And I don't even have the shaky kind of cerebral palsy.'

'Ah.'

'You're an orthopaedic surgeon. You've probably seen a thousand presentations of spastic diplegia.'

'A few, yeah,' she said. 'Although we don't rush to dorsal rhizotomy.'

'A surgeon who isn't in a rush to operate?' He sounded sceptical, and he had a fair point.

'As you said, there are so many different presentations with CP.'

'You're trying pretty hard not to make any assumptions about me.' He said it almost like a question. He was opening another bottle of bubbly, peeling away the foil covering the prosecco cork, which suddenly seemed blatantly phallic—the rounded head and long neck, or perhaps it was the way Cam was holding the bottle in his lap. 'I appreciate that.' He twisted his fist around the cork and it gave a gentle pop.

'Very smooth,' she said.

'What can I say? I get my kicks from busting stereotypes.'

Neroli leaned over towards them, passing her glass to Cam for a top-up but talking to Sasha. 'So, Northwestern in Chicago? I don't think I could handle working Emergency in the US—whole different ball game. But orthopaedics, is it much of a muchness?'

Cam was not generally a superstitious person. He didn't look for portents or put great stock in his star sign. But this had to be some kind of nudge from the universe—three times in one day—and this time she was in a shiny, figure-hugging dress with a slit he hadn't truly appreciated until she sat down in the seat beside him. The neckline was some kind of optical illusion: layers of fabric draped in a deep U-shape, all silky and soft and making him think he was seeing more than he really was.

He really shouldn't have bid on her—won her. It was just a date, he kept reminding himself. For charity. Nothing more. Why, then, could he not stop flirting with the woman?

Thankfully, his big sister could quite happily dominate the conversation with medical discussion bordering on debate. He sipped his drink and pulled his gaze away from the far too interesting woman beside him. Now the auction had finished, the dance floor filled up; the moneyed upper echelons of the medical profession were gyrating, half-cut, and halfway to doing something they'd probably regret tomorrow.

Cam would not be doing anything regrettable—at least not with anyone he might have to work with. And he would certainly be working with Sasha McBride. So this was a no-go. Not strictly against hospital rules, because she wasn't in his direct line of authority, but not a good idea. And easily avoidable.

So, that was a no, on principle alone, and then there was the rather clear *no, thank you* from the woman herself. They would get on okay as colleagues, because Cam got on with pretty much everyone. Any more than that was out of the question, no matter how much the slit revealing her bare thigh teased at his imagination.

The conversation turned from comparing medical systems to comparing whole cultures.

'It's classic tall poppy syndrome,' Neroli was saying.

Sasha replied, 'In other countries people will tell you what they're good at and keep their insecurities to themselves, but New Zealanders will brag about their flaws and casually fail to mention they're top in their field.'

Was that aimed at him? He was hardly top of his field but he *had* failed to mention he was a physio.

'The sweet potato doesn't need to say how sweet it is,' Vivian said. 'It's an old Māori proverb. But that only works in a community small enough that everyone knows how sweet everyone is.'

'And no one's new in town,' Sasha said. 'Not that I've ever been accused of saccharine—if anything, I'm too direct.'

'Better that than the alternative,' Vivian said. 'With patients, it's so important to be clear-cut.'

Cam joined in: 'And it's legally required for informed consent. People have to know what they're agreeing to, especially when they're about to be knocked out and cut open. Though interpretations vary wildly.'

'You must see a whole range.' Sasha angled towards him, crossing one leg over the other, and probably completely unaware of how much smooth, pale thigh she'd just revealed.

Very aware his sister was watching him, Cam stayed on message: 'Yeah, I see a whole…' lot of leg? 'A variety of patients and practitioners. Medical jargon goes right over people's heads, but it sounds impressive, and vulnerable patients often won't ask for clarification, but you'd be surprised how often they've no idea what you're on about.'

Neroli spoke up: 'When someone comes into ED, their bone sticking out of their leg or their life on the line, informed consent isn't always an option. We have to act fast, and explaining all the ins and outs, possible risks and complications, takes time patients cannot afford—and that's assuming they're lucid or even conscious.'

Sasha was leaning in, obviously interested in the subject matter. 'We've no such excuse with electives, but if I want to be accurate, precise, there's just no word in layman's terms for much of what I do. Sometimes "easy to understand" becomes "less than accurate". Combined with an inevitable degree of uncertainty—often in surgery we don't know until we get in there—it's easy to scare someone off a low-risk surgery that'll change their life for the better.'

'Uncertainty definitely complicates things,' Cam said.

'But it'd be dishonest to pretend certainty.' Sasha laid her hand flat on the table between them. 'Everyone wishes doctors could be more certain, could lay out cause and effect, do this, don't do this, guaranteed results. But the human body is more complex than that. And then, on the rare occasion when we actually *are* sure about something, people don't *want* to believe us.'

Cam caught her eye—she had to be talking about Joshua Tait.

She cocked her head to the side. 'I'm just saying, clear communication is not simple.'

He couldn't argue with that. It felt like an apology, the way she said it, but the truth was he'd long since forgiven—well, that was the wrong word. He didn't need to forgive anything. He understood her better now. She'd been pushy with Joshua Tait, abrupt, but she had also been clear and honest. She wanted her patient to receive the best possible care and outcomes. Cam couldn't help but admire her.

'Well, might be time for a dance,' Neroli said, and dragged Vivian away, looking back just long enough to give Cam a wink—real subtle, Sis. So his options were to stay here, chatting one-on-one with Sasha McBride, an idea he liked rather too much, or to follow his sister, making sure they all ended up dancing together. So long as he didn't pair off with the blonde temptation in the slinky dress, with the sharp mind and even sharper tongue…

No. Definitely not. He should not be thinking about her tongue.

'Dancing. Great idea,' he said and wheeled his chair back. If only there were a clear path through all the pulled-out chairs, coats and bags slung over the backs.

Neroli would usually notice, the habit of a lifetime, and clear a route for him, but she was tipsy, and apparently determined to pair him off—she'd recently reunited with Sorin, her med-school sweetheart, after years apart. How typical: the moment she was married she started on matchmaking her brother.

'Can I?' Sasha pushed in the nearest chair and indicated she would walk ahead of him.

'Ah, yeah. Thanks.'

She moved aside each and every chair in their path, bending down to pick up a dropped scarf and a scattered purse. He followed along behind her, too far gone to keep from noticing her curves in that shiny dress. 'It's like an obstacle course,' she said, crouching down to reach something—he was being tortured. 'You'd think all these medical professionals would be a little more aware.'

'I don't know,' he said, catching up to her as they joined the others on the dance floor. 'There's some pretty compelling evidence you lot are as messy as us plebs.'

'Surely you count as part of the medical profession.' She pivoted to face him, her hips finding the rhythm.

Half hypnotised, he said, 'Don't feel sorry for me. I'm a happy pleb.'

'And I thought New Zealand was less hierarchical than that,' she said, then leaned down closer and repeated herself. Maybe he'd looked confused and she'd assumed he hadn't heard her the first time, but the second time she was close enough he could catch the scent of her perfume, and the way the draping neckline of her dress fell forward. 'It's one of the things I missed, being away,' she said, 'or maybe I was just remembering this place with rose-tinted glasses.' She straightened a little.

Cam found his voice. 'It doesn't get much higher on the pecking order than a surgeon. How many letters do you put after your name?'

‘All of them.’ She grinned. ‘Because I’m a woman and it ticks people off that I’m so qualified.’

‘But you don’t like hierarchies.’

‘Nothing would happen without nurses and orderlies and cleaners and all the people relegated to the bottom of the heap. And the further up you get, the power plays, the games that come with it—just another thing that stops people saying what they really mean. I can’t stand it, but that doesn’t make it less real.’

Cam could have argued, could have said something about power coming with responsibility, but he was too busy enjoying himself—the dance, the conversation that bordered on argument, the light catching on her dress, the cadence of her voice, and the sentiment, too. She valued honesty, clarity, and so did he. Easier said than done, but this was not a woman who shied away from a challenge.

Something else they had in common.

But she was off-limits. In fact, the very reason they had all these shared values was probably the reason they did the work they did. Did she seem like a beacon of light in the dark sea of dating apps? Oh yes. Did she wave all the red flags of his past relationship disasters? Not a single one. Sasha McBride would never tell him what he wanted to hear or keep up a façade like the well-intentioned women he’d dated in the past. She’d never make idealistic assumptions about his disability—she’d ask the question and then apologise for being intrusive, and he'd never have to wonder if she saw him as some kind of charity case.

But that didn't mean she liked him. And even if she did, there was still every chance it would blow up in his face. And they had to work together. He spent most of his physio hours on her ward, and he'd certainly have advocacy work with her patients. He couldn't serve them well if he was busy crushing on their surgeon. It was a clear conflict of interest.

His sister was dancing just beside him, so he pivoted to join her, making a circle of dancers—a much safer option than pairing off. Balancing his chair on the back wheels, he was showing off, maybe just a little. But that wasn't for Sasha's benefit. That was for the sake of…dispelling a disability stereotype. Or something.

CHAPTER FOUR

In his time as a physio, Cam had worked a few different gigs. Sports medicine had been his first choice, but healthy, able-bodied patients didn't always take well to a disabled physio. And they had a tendency to push themselves, to take risks—to put it plainly, Cam wasn't great at catching people who tried to run before they could walk.

The hospital role had been a good fit from day dot, not only because hospitals were wheelchair friendly. He'd always got on well with older folks, and even his younger patients were usually cautious—something about the hospital environment slowed everyone down.

Many of his patients were recovering from hip or shoulder replacements. Cam would do their exercises with them, often earning a gasp of surprise when he rose up out of his chair. It was a good icebreaker. He'd answer their questions without forcing them to ask any: 'I have cerebral palsy, a one-off birth injury; it won't get worse, but it doesn't get much better. I can walk, but it's best for everyone if I do so sparingly. Kind of like my singing voice.

But I can't blame the CP for that.' A shared laugh, then, 'Right, Mr Williams, we're going to do something called a pendulum. You'll bend over like this, good arm supporting on the tabletop, and let your affected arm hang—it's the right one, isn't it?'

Mr Williams got up out of the reclining chair with a few groans and sighs, nothing out of the ordinary. Cam helped move the sling out of the way then stepped back to check his stance. 'Straighten your back if you can. That's better. Right, now I want you to relax that shoulder and just gently start moving in a small circle.' Cam demonstrated. Mr Williams swung his arm in tiny circles, but it was a start.

Cam straightened and noticed they weren't alone—Sasha was standing in the doorway. 'Good morning,' she said. 'How are you feeling, Mr Williams?'

'Like my arm might just fall off.'

'I promise it won't,' she said.

Cam put one hand just beyond the circle Mr Williams' hand was drawing. 'A little wider. Just to here. That's the one. Now can you reverse it—anticlockwise this time?'

'Have you just started?' Sasha asked Cam.

'Yeah, but I can come back if you need…'

'No, no.' She looked at her tablet, perhaps at Mr Williams' notes. 'Two days post-op, how's your pain, George?'

'Comes and goes.' He stood up and went a little pale.

'Have a seat,' Cam said. 'The next exercise is sitting down.'

'You can have some more ibuprofen in an hour,' Sasha said. 'I popped by yesterday but you were sleeping. Just wanted to check if you had any questions.'

He shook his head.

'Mind if I observe?' Sasha asked.

'Depends what he wants me doing next,' Mr Williams said.

'Don't worry.' Cam sat back in his wheelchair and rolled it right up beside the recliner. 'Nothing too extreme today.'

Cam took him through assisted forward arm elevation, passive rotations and finally some shoulder-blade movements. Cam usually did all the movements himself, keeping a slow and steady pace for his patients, and giving his own body the gentle movements his often tight muscles needed. But with Sasha watching, he was self-conscious. On the dance floor, just five days ago, he'd been easy, fully aware she was looking at him, bold and inviting. Flirting, half arguing, and then loosely planning a date, even though there would never be more than one. Blame the prosecco, but he'd been far too relaxed then. Now, not even a little bit.

Cam's attention was supposed to be on Mr Williams, checking he was doing the movements correctly and not in too much pain.

But he didn't have to look at Sasha to know she was looking at him—he could feel her gaze on him.

They went out into the hallway together, leaving Mr Williams with four exercises to do three times a day.

'Thanks for letting me observe,' Sasha said.

'No problem.'

'It's helpful to know. I wouldn't want to contradict a colleague.'

'What, are the physios in Chicago giving them handstands and high fives?'

She laughed. 'No, it's mostly the same, but I like to be sure.'

'Well, I'm off to do hip abductions and extensions with Gail Travers in room nine if you're interested.' Not that Cam particularly wanted Sasha watching him struggle to straighten his leg.

'I have two others to stop in on first, but I may well see you there.' Sasha met his gaze for a long beat. Was that in his head? Was time slowing down? He was far too willing to imagine she felt something, because he did. No use denying it, at least not to himself. But this was an ordinary day's work and they'd be crossing paths twice in an hour. She wasn't his boss, not technically, but the mere fact he was considering technicalities said it all: this one-off date was going to be low-key torture.

Sasha peeked through the window of Mrs Travers' door and watched Cam work. He was perched on the side of a raised hospital bed, holding the older woman's hand. In sync, the pair rocked forward onto their feet and rose to standing. He was so patient, a smile on his face, speaking just quietly enough that Sasha couldn't hear any words, even though the door was open. But she could hear his tone—the warmth, care, humour.

Sasha cared about her patients, too, it just didn't come out in every word like that; it wasn't written all over her face and baked into her body language. Mind you, as she was a surgeon, most of her patients weren't conscious, so perhaps it didn't matter as much. But he made it look easy, and she couldn't help but envy that.

Sasha shouldn't be hanging about in the hallway. If she didn't get through all these post-op check-ins on schedule, she'd pay for it later, but she couldn't seem to help herself. His slow and steady movements sparked her curiosity about his mobility. A week ago she'd have been more curious about his patients' responses to his chair, but clearly that wasn't an issue—or he was so practiced at dealing with it, a pithy explanation ready to go, word for word. All he'd told Sasha was that it was spastic diplegia. He'd basically complimented her for not making assumptions, but he'd volunteered very little. He was probably sick of explaining his private medical condition to strangers, and Sasha wouldn't want to be just another nosy stranger.

A stranger he'd danced with, had a few drinks with, flirted with—she was almost certain he'd been flirting—and they were going out next weekend.

So not really a stranger. But it was none of her

business how he managed his patients, even if many of them were also her patients.

'You can come in,' he said.

'Oh, Dr McBride.' Mrs Travers looked over. 'Can I go home this afternoon? My son is coming to stay with me for a few days, so he'll help.'

'Let's see, shall we?' Sasha pulled up Mrs Travers' notes and saw the nurses' records—temperature, blood pressure, heart rate. Steady and promising for the most part. 'Mind if I observe your physio session?'

Mrs Travers gave a sigh—an objection to the exercises themselves, rather than the observation. 'What's next, then?' she asked Cam.

'Hip extensions, then we'll go for a walk, maybe find some stairs.'

With a gentle grumble, she held tight to the bed frame and extended her leg backwards. Cam did the same, clearly with little more ease than his patient.

'I know it's not easy,' he said. 'Three, two, one, release. This is why I had you do the lying-down sets first. At home, you want to be warmed up before you stand up.'

'I know,' she said.

Cam moved the walker in front of her. 'Lead the way, Mrs Travers.' He went to his chair.

'You're not walking with me this time?'

'I'm coming with you, just not walking. I've done my exercises for the day.'

'What are you going to do when we get to the stairs?' she asked.

'Are you planning an escape? I don't often have to chase a patient.'

'Maybe I'd better come just in case,' Sasha said, glad of the excuse, thin though it was—Mrs Travers would be doing well to go up three steps and down again. The attempt might make her less eager to go home, and, given the woman's age and blood pressure, Sasha would encourage another day's in-patient care.

They made slow progress down the hallway. Sasha could feel the time clawing at her—she shouldn't be here, but there was something about Cam, his gentle cajoling and easy humour. The stairwell was behind a heavy smoke-stop door. He hauled it open and pivoted his chair to act as a door-stop, leaving just enough room for Mrs Travers and her walker. 'Now, no running off. I see you eyeing the exit signs,' Cam teased. Sasha found herself wishing he were talking to her.

'I should get back to…' She caught Cam's eye, the question there, curious and far too observant, as though he knew she was playing hooky just to hang out with him, as though he saw right through her. 'I'll come by later and see about that early discharge, Mrs Travers.'

Cam was in half an hour before his shift started because one of his outpatients was scheduled for surgery and having second thoughts. And because he was a sucker sometimes. Hard to say no to someone about to have back surgery.

Plenty of reasons to be there early, and none of them were about Sasha McBride. Even if she was his patient's surgeon.

For the past year, Gemma Edie's C7 vertebra had caused her an enormous amount of pain and none of the non-invasive treatments were working. Months of trying various therapies, steroid injections, medications, getting her hopes up, getting a little relief for a while—the roller coaster of it all had left her fragile, uncertain, exhausted.

So it was no great surprise that four minutes after he arrived her stoic expression had slipped. He handed over the tissues and listened to her ask questions about the surgery that he simply couldn't answer.

'How about we talk to the surgeon?' he suggested.

Gemma nodded. 'I think the bit that's really freaking me out is this robot thing she wants to use. Just the thought of a robot cutting me open and, I don't know, shaving off bits of my spine—I mean, it's bad enough, but the fact it's a robot—you know what I mean?'

'Shall I see if I can find Dr McBride?'

'Okay.'

Pre-op was far more cold, hard and sterile than the orthopaedic ward. They'd probably have fewer patients in a last-minute panic if the place felt a little cosier.

Sasha came around a corner. 'Cam, what are you doing down here?'

'Looking for you, as it happens.'

'I have surgery in ten minutes.'

'Yeah, I've been working with Gemma Edie in Outpatients for a while and she asked me to come in. She has some questions.'

'Is she changing her mind about the surgery?'

'No, I don't think so, but some reassurance wouldn't go amiss.'

Sasha wasn't exactly surprised to find her patient teary and exhausted. The surprise was Cam McColl rolling in beside her as if he'd done this a thousand times.

'Good morning, how are we doing?' Sasha felt silly even saying it—the answer was obviously not great.

Gemma gave a watery smile, the huff of an almost-laugh.

'Perfectly normal to feel emotional,' Sasha said.

'I just wish it was over already.' Gemma smushed a tissue into her nose. 'I just want my life back.'

'I know. That's why we're all here.' Sasha pulled up a chair. 'So, we talked through the surgery at our last appointment, but if you have any questions now, that's why I'm here.'

Gemma turned to Cam, clearly someone she trusted or he wouldn't be here to begin with, but all he had to do was nod and give a reassuring smile—that was all it took and Gemma's shoulders dropped. Weirdly, even though it wasn't directed at her, Sasha too felt a little less worried. As if they were all in safe hands. As if this physio would iron out all the wrinkles and everything would be fine. What was it about this guy? Did he give off some kind of disarming pheromone? Not that he always put Sasha at ease, in fact quite the opposite, but that was clearly his goal now and it was like magic.

He said, 'She's a bit unsure about the robotic assistance you're wanting to use in the surgery.'

Sasha turned to Gemma. 'Is that correct?'

Gemma nodded, sniffing and blotting her eyes. 'The idea of a robot, it's getting in my head. I haven't been sleeping very well, and my brain just goes all over the show.'

'That's not uncommon before a surgery,' Sasha said.

'Can it just be you? No robot?'

Sasha nodded, because, yeah, it was technically possible for her to do this surgery the way she'd been doing it—the way everyone had been doing it—for decades. 'The thing is, for someone like you, Gemma, generally healthy and active, with a good understanding of your condition and great support at home, we really want to get you in and out of hospital as soon as possible—and I know you want that too. Robotic assistance means a smaller incision, less room for error, and we don't need to do imaging during your surgery, so we won't expose you to radioactivity.'

'But I've already had MRIs and CT scans.'

'But less is better. The robotic assistant gives me a much better view of your vertebra and the surrounding tissues, it improves accuracy beyond any human capability, and reduces risks of complications. You'll have less chance of infection or further surgery.'

'Yeah, I read the information you gave me about all that,' Gemma said.

'It seems to me you're a really good candidate.'

'I just don't understand what the robot does. Surely you can use a…what do you call it? A laparoscopic camera? Without needing a whole robotic thing to do the actual surgery.'

'The placement of the pedicle screws is the main difference.'

Gemma visibly shuddered at the mention of screws, and Sasha probably should have seen that coming. Informed consent really could be a double-edged sword. Telling patients exactly what was about to happen to them was a quick way to stress out anyone not chomping sedatives. Not to mention that stress was bad for the immune system.

Cam wheeled his chair around, shifting the angle so he was facing Gemma, but he spoke to Sasha. 'Is there an alternative?'

'Yes, but it increases your chances of needing a second operation.'

'My friend's mum had this surgery,' Gemma said. 'She didn't have to have two operations, and there was no robot involved.'

'Robotic assistance is relatively new,' Sasha said.

'Wouldn't something tried and true be better?'

Gemma asked. The logic was understandable, if flawed.

But when it came to this specific surgery, Sasha was one of the most experienced orthopaedic surgeons in the country. 'It's relatively new technology here in New Zealand, but I've been working with it in the States for five years. I've participated in over a hundred of these surgeries, and I cannot in good conscience recommend a conventional fluoroscopy-assisted placement or freehand technique.'

The silence was palpable. Sasha caught Cam's eye—no gentle humour and curious flirting now. She remembered their conversation about medical jargon at the fundraiser. And here she was being all kinds of hypocritical.

'Fluoroscopy is with imaging, like an X-ray, and freehand is—'

'I get it,' Gemma said. 'I'm just nervous and exhausted. Let's do this.'

Sasha checked on her tablet that the consent form had been all done—she didn't want to risk delaying that, but it was already completed. 'Okay, we're good to go. I'll see you soon.'

Cam followed her out into the corridor. 'Dr McBride. Sasha. Come on.'

'What?'

He wheeled along a bit further, out of their patient's hearing perhaps, then pivoted on the spot to face her. 'You can do it without the robotic assist. She clearly isn't comfortable.'

'She's consented. We've been over it. I'm giving

her the best care, the safest procedure, the fastest possible recovery. There's no downside.'

'Except she's feeling pressured to go ahead with something she doesn't want.'

'She wants her life back, and this is the best way to give her that. She only needs reassurance,' Sasha said, and hoped Cam would get the message: *go back in there and work your magic*. She'd seen him on the ward plenty this week: reassurance was his superpower. 'It's perfectly normal to be nervous before an operation. Speaking of which, I need to scrub in. Excuse me.'

Cam didn't usually let a terse interaction with a doctor play over and over in his head. He was used to bruising the odd ego, was generally very comfortable with being a pain in the arse if that was what it took to do his job properly.

But Sasha McBride had really got under his skin. He'd had hours now and still hadn't put his finger on exactly why that was. He had plenty to keep him busy—a full schedule of appointments, post-operative assessments for hip and shoulder replacements, a few knees and ACLs, one ankle reconstruction. His unscheduled visit with Gemma had him running late, rushing to catch up all day. But he was finally getting a break—he could check in on Gemma in Recovery, put his mind at ease.

Sasha had been resolute, committed to the surgical option she preferred—even if she was right, and she probably was, that robotic assistance was the safest, fastest and all-round best option, the patient had had real concerns. And Sasha hadn't genuinely offered the alternative path. That was what bugged Cam. Not that he'd been the one to tell her off—and now there was something between them, air they would need to clear at some point.

Gemma was out of surgery, so that was a good sign it had all gone as expected, but she was still unconscious. Cam had looked in all the usual places, but Sasha was nowhere to be found. Dr Vivian Stirling, the head of Orthopaedics, spotted him across the recovery ward. 'We don't usually see you here. Everything all right?'

'Yeah, this is one of mine.' He pointed to Gemma. 'I'd hoped to catch Dr McBride.'

Dr Stirling's expression barely altered, but he could see the interest and amusement—she thought he had a crush, that he was making excuses to cross paths with Sasha.

'I just had some concerns about the…' What was he doing? Telling on her to the boss? No, that would really be crossing a line. 'The robotic assistance—I just wanted to check I understood, for future reference. In case I get questions.'

'Sasha's the expert there. It's half the reason we hired her.' Vivian came right up to Gemma's bedside. 'This was a great teaching case—lots of interest from other departments observing. But instead of hanging around afterwards for some well-earned praise and adulation, our Sasha took an emergency consult, and then I think she went home for the day.'

Right. So Cam would have to wait to clear the air another time. But that wasn't why he was here anyway—he was here to make sure that Gemma woke up to a friendly face.

CHAPTER FIVE

SASHA HAD BEEN staring at her wardrobe door for way longer than she could possibly justify. Cam had sent a text message an hour ago, saying only, Are we still on for the basketball?

Was it her imagination or was he looking for an out?

She'd replied, Yeah, looking forward to it.

He'd sent her the address, a link to the map online, and nothing else.

What did one wear to the basketball here? She'd been to a few games in Chicago, all part of the cultural experience, living in America, but everything was more low-key here. Jeans and boots. It'd probably be warm inside the stadium. Maybe just a tee shirt. Casual but cute.

Sasha didn't need to over-think this. One date, just colleagues with a side of potential friendship. He'd bid on her because it was for a good cause, and probably because his sister had talked him into it, and maybe to mend things after that almost-argument about Mr Tait on her first day.

See you there, Sasha typed in—cool and casual.

The exact opposite of how she was feeling. Because they'd had another almost-argument just before Gemma Edie's surgery, and that was the last she'd seen him. If it weren't for the text messages, she'd be worried he might not show up.

No, that wasn't fair. Cam was a good guy; he wouldn't stand her up.

Sasha looked at the bus options—all doable, but she was too nervous to deal with the added blow to her confidence that would come with getting lost en route. So she called a taxi.

'I could have dropped you off on the way to my dinner,' her sister said. She was perched at the kitchen counter, sharing a bowl of popcorn with Mya, who was chuffed to have the house to herself for the evening, was *only having a couple of friends over*, and had very successfully derailed all attempts at further questioning by dishing the gossip on all her friends' parents' divorces.

'You look so pretty,' Mya said to Sasha. 'Oh my God, those boots are boss.'

That boost carried Sasha all the way to the stadium—well, by American standards it probably wouldn't even qualify as a stadium. More like an oversized school gymnasium than a major sporting venue. She had that awful feeling she might be in the wrong place, but the taxi had already left, so in she went.

Inside, the place was lit up and warm; music played and the crowd buzzed with excitement. Maybe it would all be fine.

She looked for Cam along the bottom of the bleachers. There were several wheelchairs, but he wasn't in any of them. That was when it hit her—this was wheelchair basketball. She'd just assumed. She should know better.

And then she spotted Neroli, Cam's sister, waving her over as though she'd been expecting no one else, looking for Sasha.

What was going on?

Cam made his way towards her, weaving through the people on the edge of the courts. He was in full kit as if he were about to play the game, not watch it. Must be a serious fan, then, and why not? Disgusted with herself, she said, 'I don't have any merch yet. Do they sell it here or is it online?'

'Online I think, but… I've been roped in to play. Some of the team are unwell, and I play in this league, so they asked me to step in, to make up numbers.'

'Oh. Right. But your sister's here.'

'Yeah, her kid is right into basketball, so I got him season tickets for his birthday.'

It all made perfect sense. So why did she feel as though she was being let down easy?

Cam was giving the warm-up his complete attention. Every stretch, every rep, he counted movements and breaths, felt his muscles activate. He needed all the help he could get right now. It was the sort-of-a-date nerves. It was the unresolved question of their conversation outside Gemma Edie's room.

It was the slap-upside-the-head attraction—Sasha's jeans hugged her hips and that tee shirt stretched across her chest then hung loose everywhere else as though it wasn't an intentional thing, that being that sexy was just accidental. Effortless. Her blonde hair was down, loose curls and glinting earrings peeking between and snapping his attention back to her, as if there were any danger of his focus fixing on anything else in the world.

Cam knew better than most that physical well-being couldn't be separated from the mental and emotional stuff. If he was frustrated, worried, tense…all of that landed in his body. He'd carry it with him, up and down the court. It would slow his reflexes and knock his balance.

Outside his not-quite-having-it body, the stadium was pumping with energy. The stands were filling up. He loved to see it—to see people come out on a Friday night for wheelchair basketball, just as they did for the non-wheelchair kind. Society in general was getting better in a lot of ways. Here was reason to stay hopeful. On one hand, Sasha McBride might yet prove to be as pushy and arrogant as too many surgeons before her, but on the other, an endless stream of people was filing into the old stadium, clambering up the bleachers.

He needed to put Sasha out of his head, just for a little while. The game needed to be a no-Sasha zone. He scooped up a basketball, volleyed it back and forth between his hands, felt the imprint rough and secure in his grip. He was in control of the ball.

And of his thoughts. That slinky purple dress with the slit right up her thigh—no. He dropped the ball in his lap and pivoted his chair, felt the wheels skim against his fingers, the heat of friction, the movement precise and intentional. He was in control. He was.

He spotted Sasha sitting down with his sister in the crowd. Neroli was introducing her to her husband and son. Cam gave them a wave. Jules, his nephew, waved back, clearly uninterested in Sasha, and two things struck Cam with equal force. One: the idea of anyone finding Sasha uninteresting was utterly baffling. Two: they made quite the picture, all sitting together like a family. It'd be nice, to have someone come watch his games, cheer him on, celebrate or commiserate as the case might be, afterwards; someone who got on with his sister and his family and wanted in—wanted to be his person.

Truth was, every time he'd got his hopes up, they'd proved him wrong. Every time Cam had thought he'd met someone who might fit in that picture… Beth had wanted him to be something he wasn't. And he'd wanted Lily to be something she wasn't. And Twyla…it was probably a bit of both in that case. The one time he'd dated another medical professional—thank God her physiotherapy clinic was private—she didn't work at the hospital.

But Sasha did. And if he'd learned anything from the whole Twyla debacle it was that assuming the best of people was a risky venture.

* * *

The ball went up. Basketball was always fun to watch: fast, dynamic, plenty of points and turnovers, never a dull moment. Sasha had only seen wheelchair basketball on TV, never live. What would Cam say to that? Thankfully, he never needed to know.

She watched him play, watched him manoeuvre his way up the court, his arms, his hands, quick and strong, action and reaction, pivot and pull. Was the whole crowd leaning forward in their seats or was that just her? Hungry to be a little closer. Anxious not to miss a beat.

He snatched the ball with the very tips of his fingers. It really looked as if it'd bounce right off, but it curled back into his reach. The look on his face, the lift and dread and relief—Sasha felt everything she witnessed as though there was some kind of cosmic link between them.

'Not exactly the date you were promised,' Neroli said, something like concern in her voice.

Sasha hated to think what her facial expressions had been giving away. 'I don't mind. It's cool he was able to jump in—I mean, not *jump*, but you know what I mean.'

Neroli laughed. 'Yeah, not as much jumping in this league.'

'And it's the principle of the thing.'

'What is?' Neroli asked.

'This date. It's for charity. It's not like a real one. Not that I'd object if it were, but I'm pretty sure he didn't mean it like that.'

Neroli just looked at her as if she'd sprouted wings.

'I'm new at the hospital. I don't know anyone. He's just being friendly.'

'Sure, yeah, and a complete muppet.'

'What?'

'He's a muppet.'

'Like Kermit?'

'Like a chaos show. Twyla did a freakin' number on him. Well, not just Twyla. Don't tell him I told you about Twyla. It's not like they were the real deal.'

'Neroli,' Sorin said out of the corner of his mouth in a tone that said, *maybe say less?*

'Anyway,' Neroli said, 'if you want this to be a real date, trust me, he's not opposed. He's just a muppet.'

Out on the court, Cam spun on the spot, just as he had in the corridor outside Gemma Edie's room, questioning the woman's consent. At the time, Sasha had been in the zone, focused on the task ahead, but in the days that had followed she hadn't seen Cam on the ward, and maybe it was all this nervous energy and attraction, her own insecurities and Liam's voice in her head, but she did wonder—would he have questioned a male surgeon in the same way? Women in medicine were forever getting pulled up for being direct and confident and having the sheer audacity to be an expert. Men in the same roles were applauded for taking such good care of their patients, for being so trustworthy and clearly knowing what they were doing. Boldness was admirable and reassuring in men but off-putting in women. Certainty earned men promotions while women like Sasha got 'difficult' reputations.

So she'd used a little jargon—she'd immediately explained. And the surgery had gone incredibly well. Gemma was far better off this way. Sasha had been *right*.

Cam fumbled a quick catch and release, flicking the ball outside the boundary line. Shoulders slumping, he let his head fall back, frustration writ large in his posture. Beside Sasha, Neroli jumped to her feet and shouted, 'You got this, Cam!' She clapped her hands. 'You got this!'

Cam turned towards them as Sorin and Jules got up. Sasha was a moment later, but stood and clapped. He seemed to be looking right at her, his eyes sharp but uncertain. She remembered his words, arguing about Gemma's surgery, *she's feeling pressured...she clearly isn't comfortable... Sasha...come on.* Cam's pleading, his passion, enough to give her pause.

Then he gave a weak smile and pivoted back to the play.

And Sasha watched, her body tighter by the minute with undeniable attraction, her mind fraught with the tangle of their every interaction. The way he moved, the ripple of muscle, the confidence of every clash with his opponents, the way he swiped his hair back off his face, called out to his teammates. He gave his whole being so entirely to the game, it all made her light up with desire, wound tight, imagination run wild—those hands, that mouth, those arms.

And it didn't matter how many times she told herself it wasn't going to happen, that this wasn't a real date, that he didn't even like her. That only made her want him more.

CHAPTER SIX

THE FINAL BUZZER ended the game and Cam's relief lasted a fraction of a second.

Now what? Was Sasha about to congratulate him on a great—but honestly not that great—game? Were they going out for drinks and a bite to eat, playing this like a date? Physically, he was wiped out, but endorphins and a quick shower would soon fix that. Mentally and emotionally, he was going to struggle—struggle to bite his tongue, to keep his feelings under wraps, keep it casual, when what he really wanted to do was argue with her or kiss her. Put some safe distance between them…or none at all.

Jules ran across the court shouting, 'Nice shot, Uncle Cam. That steal was savage!'

Cam put up his hand for the high five, but he was looking past his teenage nephew. Sasha was saying something to his sister. She was leaving. Disappointment churned in his gut. Regret. She'd come tonight expecting to watch the game *with him*; maybe he should have checked in with her before agreeing to play. Or had Neroli said something?

Jules had picked up a stray basketball, and Sorin was shooting hoops with him. Neroli strolled up. 'Well done,' she said. 'Snatched victory from the jaws of defeat.'

He shook his head. 'It was almost snatching defeat from the jaws of victory. Not my best game.'

'All worked out in the end.' She glanced towards the exit, where Sasha had disappeared moments earlier—Cam's peripheral vision refused not to notice. 'Aren't the hardest-fought battles the most satisfying wins?'

'Are you talking about basketball or…?'

Neroli smirked. 'Where are you taking her?'

'Am I taking her anywhere?'

'Are you serious? The self-sabotage.'

'I'm not sabotaging anything. She just left, didn't she?'

'She went to the bathroom.'

'Oh. Right. Well, in that case.'

Sorin joined them. 'Good game.'

Cam only nodded his thanks.

'We'll get out of your hair,' Sorin said, putting his arm loosely about Neroli's shoulders.

'Unless you want us to come,' Neroli said.

'No, I think I'll manage from here,' Cam said, half relief, half something else entirely. He watched the trio walk out, and then Sasha was coming back in, right towards him, an absolute vision. Was he really about to take this woman out and give it zero chances of meaning anything?

'Good game,' she said.

'Thanks.' He wheeled over, meeting her halfway across the court. 'I got us a table at a little place around the corner. I'll just have a quick shower and get changed.'

'Sounds good.' She pushed her hands into her pockets, the first clue she was feeling as nervous as he was. Nice to know it wasn't just him…but he didn't want her nervous. He wanted her to have a nice time, to like him, to not rule him out prematurely.

So maybe he should do the same for her—keep an open mind.

Sasha reapplied her lipstick, again. He'd booked them a table. Could she ignore the nagging question and enjoy the evening, let it be whatever it would be? Not exactly her forte. Curiosity and speaking her mind mostly served her well. Her hunger to learn, to understand, was central to her every achievement, and a lot of that came down to asking the damn question.

But this wasn't a medical anomaly or innovative technology. This wasn't a rare presentation or a new technique. This was attraction and mixed messages. This was probably a terrible idea, an unnecessary complication with a colleague—and shouldn't she have learned that lesson after Liam?

But she liked Cam. And she had to know if there was something there.

An answer to the question. And if that answer

was 'thanks, but no, thanks' she could at least draw a line under this whole thing. That would be that.

Cam came out of the changing rooms in a crisp shirt, his hair still wet, face still flushed, eyes searching for her. The stadium had almost emptied out, but Sasha wasn't the only one waiting for a player to emerge. She stood up and, the moment his gaze landed on her, she felt that physically.

'All set?' she asked. Why was she breathless all of a sudden?

'All set,' he answered.

They weren't even out of the door before she broke: 'Just to be clear, this doesn't have to be a *date* date. I'm… Either way. But no pressure.'

'No pressure,' he repeated.

She caught his gaze but his expression gave nothing away.

Outside he gestured towards the road and the direction they'd take, the restaurant he'd chosen for the occasion. A few silent moments later, he said, 'The thing is, we're going to be seeing a lot of each other.'

'Exactly.'

'It's probably simpler if we don't…'

'Undeniably,' Sasha said, but her disappointment was likely written all over her face. Thankfully, in the deep dusk, Cam probably didn't notice.

'We can just have a meal and…'

Sasha offered, 'And continue working together.'

'Exactly.' There was something about the way he said the word, though. It tugged at her, made her wonder what exactly had happened with this Twyla person Neroli had mentioned. Sasha's curiosity, that hungry beast, was piqued. And a little ticked off—someone had hurt this guy, had given him reason to hold back and protect himself.

The restaurant was in an old villa. Twinkling lights led them around the house, up a mossy path to a brick courtyard. Lush ferns and fragrant herbs made it feel like The Secret Garden from the novel.

'This is gorgeous,' Sasha said.

'Are you warm enough to sit outside?' Cam asked her.

She nodded, and maybe she'd regret it later, but right now she was plenty warm—nerves, attraction, the brisk walk—plus this garden was straight out of a fairy tale. Music wafted from indoors, a familiar tune, a silky voice. This was perfect.

The shower had helped. The conversation on the walk over…not so much. He should feel relieved: they were on the same page, this wasn't a date, this was just colleagues being friendly. No complications. No risk.

'You'd never guess this was hidden away here,' Sasha said. 'One of those places only the locals know about?'

'Word has spread now—it's usually busier. I guess we're after the dinner rush.'

'True.'

Into the lull, he said what he'd been meaning to say earlier: 'Sorry about the change of plans—

not exactly what you thought you were getting this evening.'

'It's fine. Neroli's great.'

'But not especially subtle.'

She met his gaze over the wine list. 'No, not subtle, but it's kind of nice. I mean, you're clearly close. That's nice.'

'She's in the honeymoon phase with Sorin, so she wants everyone else to…' be just as happy and loved-up as she was. It wasn't that Cam didn't want those things, but it was different for Sorin and Neroli; they'd clicked from the day they'd met. And sure, it had all fallen apart, but they weren't starting from scratch. They knew one another, really knew one another, knew exactly what they were getting into—knew it was worth the risk.

'Did you set them up?' Sasha asked.

'No. If anything, the opposite.' The words just slipped out, but now he'd have to explain. She'd arched an eyebrow and everything.

'What's the opposite of setting her up? He seems a nice guy.'

'He is. It wasn't on purpose, but I did break them up—fifteen years ago, I mean. She's the responsible eldest child, the looker-afterer. So when the love of her life took off to the other side of the world, rather than go with him, she stayed here.'

'Because of you?'

'I'd just had surgery.'

'Okay, but not by choice, I'm guessing.'

'Does it matter?' Was he really about to point

out all the ways his disability, and all the risks that went with it, might impact on his family, his loved ones…anyone who tied themselves to him?

Sasha said, 'It wasn't like you chose to keep her here, to need the support.'

'I could have told her to go. Back then, I wasn't the confident professional you see before you today, arguing with top surgeons in the hallways.' It was a segue, a shameless pivot from this too-revealing conversation to another topic—perhaps just as awkward.

'Top surgeons can handle it,' Sasha said, as though it were nothing.

As though it hadn't bothered her at all; meanwhile, he'd been going in circles about it all day. 'I stopped in on Gemma in Recovery. Stirling said it went well.'

'Yeah, I was happy with it. I'll go see her tomorrow. Gemma, I mean. Probably Vivian, too. She's lining up surgeons from other specialties to observe any and all robotic-assisted procedures. I know what I'm doing in the room, but I'm not great at the sales pitch.' She put down the menu and it slapped shut with a certain finality. 'As you're aware.'

'I don't know if it's helpful to frame it as a sales pitch,' he said.

That was when the server arrived, pausing their conversation at peak awkward to espouse the fish of the day and suggest the mulled wine. There was just enough chill in the air for a warm drink to sell itself.

Sasha spoke as soon as the server left them. 'I don't actually think of it as a sales pitch. That's not what I meant.'

'No?'

'I don't have your, ah, talent for reassuring people, for picking up on all the nuances of their anxiety.'

'I mostly just listen,' Cam said. 'Listen and repeat things, rephrase, check for understanding.'

The mulled wine arrived, glasses steaming, bright crescents of orange bobbing beneath the surface. Sasha touched her fingertips to the glass as if checking the temperature, graceful and cautious at once—those hands were precision instruments.

She sighed and said, 'It's a fine line, going into detail about surgical procedures with patients. Anything more than a broad-strokes description is just confusing and alarming. Heck, I'd be worried if the general population *weren't* alarmed by the idea of cutting someone open and grinding away portions of bone.'

'Fair,' Cam said, and took a sip of his mulled wine—fragrant, a little spicy, a little sweet. The kind of drink one might forget contained alcohol. It would go down very smoothly. Much like everything Sasha was saying. How easily he might forget himself. He grasped at the argument. 'But you have a responsibility to ensure patients fully understand what they're consenting to.'

'Absolutely. But good luck defining "fully understand". If I start describing bone saws and chisels, no one will ever undergo orthopaedic surgery ever again. So we sanitise the language, we *remove* a piece of bone. I'm saying more about the robotic assistant than I ever did about any other surgical instrument—maybe that's the issue. I should say less.'

'I get that it's a fine line, but if you want my opinion…'

'I do.' She leaned in close. She was interested in what he was saying, listening. Really listening. And chewing the inside her lip—he was close enough to see the point of her canine drag against the soft flesh.

'I think you should trust your patients to be competent adults who can decide for themselves. It's less about what you say, more about listening to what *they're* saying. Or not saying.'

'You think I'm being condescending?'

'I think acting in your patients' best interests isn't always black and white.'

'No kidding.'

'I think we can all learn a lot from each other.'

She nodded to that, her expression one of deep thought. All that careful consideration of what he'd said—maybe he shouldn't be so easily impressed, but he was. Impressed. Borderline hypnotised by her mouth, too—every sip of her drink, lick of her lips.

'It's weird, coming back to Christchurch, back

home,' she said. 'When I left, I was basically still a teenager. We didn't hang out at places like this.'

'No, it was all skate parks and malls,' Cam said.

'Exactly. It's quite the mental adjustment. I'm looking at apartments tomorrow and my sister recommended a bougie brunch place nearby.'

'Which one?'

'Well, exactly—that's my point. There are so many of them. This is not the Christchurch I left behind.'

They were still talking about bougie brunch places when the dinner arrived.

Sasha had to bite her tongue to keep from inviting him to go with her tomorrow. It'd be so easy. The conversation had carried her all the way to it, but they'd agreed this was just a meal. And planning a second date, especially the very next day, would blur that line.

So, she told him about the two different apartments and the one little old villa she was considering renting.

'What's the accessibility like?' he asked.

'One of them has a lift,' she said, but beyond that she hadn't really given it any thought. 'Isn't there a shortage of accessible rental accommodation? Shouldn't I leave to those who need it?'

The food was delicious, but no buttery sauce nor herby potato rosti would keep her from registering Cam's reaction—she'd said the wrong thing. His face went all strained and uncertain, his eyes darkening. 'What is it?' she asked.

'The higher the demand—if people want it—then more rental properties will provide. Plus, you might have a guest.'

'True.' And painfully obvious, now he said it. How had she not considered…? Was she doomed to always say the wrong thing with this guy? Always getting the wrong end of the stick. Or giving him the wrong end of the…okay, unhelpful analogy. 'You ever get tired of pointing out what should be blatantly obvious to people who should know better?'

He smiled, and it felt like so much more than she deserved.

The server came back. 'Another drink?'

'Why not?' Sasha said, and there was something about saying the question out loud—why not get a drink with this guy? Because Cam was too tempting, too warm and quick and generous. Everything she wasn't. All her cold, prickly edges were supposed to scare off anyone who'd want her to be anything else. Why not have a drink with this guy and loosen up and maybe ditch an inhibition or two? Because then he'd see her for what she was: too much, that was what Liam had said. She was too much. Too driven, too outspoken, too certain, too exacting, too focused, too critical, too sensitive. And for all that, she was left feeling as though she wasn't good enough.

But Cam wasn't Liam. Cam was a very different person.

So if Sasha let him see beneath the surface and he found her wanting in the very same way, then it wasn't about Liam at all. If Cam saw the same thing in her, then it was *her*. It was true.

And then he would stop looking at her like that. The way he was looking at her right now: as if she were dinner and he were hungry.

This was a foolish line of thought. Sasha wasn't interested in any man who wanted her to be something she wasn't. As nice as it was to be wanted, she would only be disappointed in the end. Again. So she would be herself, let the chips fall where they may, and try not to do anything she'd regret.

'I'm curious,' Cam said. 'Why orthopaedics?'

Fair question, but she didn't have a clear-cut answer.

'Did you ever break a bone?' he asked.

'Nothing serious—fell off the monkey bars in primary school, did my tibia.' Sasha was watching the star anise swirl in her glass, because holding his eye contact was feeling like a lot. It was nice to be seen, sure, but she wasn't used to this level of attention. He was so…interested. But not pushy, not at all. He asked a question then sat back and let her answer, as if he had no plans here, no expectations. Maybe he genuinely didn't want anything from her. He was a friendly guy.

She was nothing special; he was just being nice.

* * *

Cam watched her expression falter, open one moment, holding back the next. This smart, beautiful, infuriating woman, this temptation in tight jeans, and what was that scent when she leaned closer? Like blossoms and fresh air, coconut and sunlight. She was bright as spring, and if they didn't work together, he wouldn't hesitate.

'For one thing,' she said, 'orthopaedics has a low mortality rate. And there's something very satisfying about it, figuring out the best solution—we do the same procedure a hundred times but every case is different. I find it fascinating. Not to mention all the incredible innovations and new technology. It's like engineering but for human bodies.'

Her hand brushed his mid-gesture. A momentary touch and she immediately pulled back, as though she hadn't meant it at all. But even that brief press, nothing at all between her smooth skin and his, just heat and a shiver of potential. The teasing heat of wanting her. The post-game endorphins were still pumping in his system—was that why he was so willing to abandon his resolution? This was one meal, one and done, not the start of anything other than professional camaraderie. But when she put her glass down, he let his hand brush hers briefly. Their eyes met.

There was a question there in her expression. She wanted to ask something. She was holding back.

'What is it?' he asked.

'This is okay?' she said.

In answer, he grazed his knuckles against the back of her hand, and when she didn't pull away, he hooked a finger around two of hers, tugged her closer, tilting his head, thinking about—but not *actually*—kissing her, and she had to know what he was thinking.

The look on her face said she was probably thinking about it, too.

'What time's your viewing tomorrow?' he asked her.

'Viewing? Oh, the apartment. Nine-thirty. But I should have another look at the listing, check the accessibility. I can't believe I hadn't considered…'

He could believe it, but he didn't want to think about that now. There was something so delicious about this wanting, about her closeness; he could almost taste her. He was holding her hand—she was holding his right back.

So, she had her blind spots. Who didn't? The fact she wanted to know about them was huge. That she'd guessed he might get tired of pointing out ablism when it should be obvious—God, it felt good for someone to get that, to understand without him having to spell it out. He wasn't blind to her faults, but that didn't make him like her any less… No danger of this woman telling him only what he wanted to hear, keeping her true feelings hidden, like women he'd dated before. If he'd learned anything from the crash and burn of those fledgling relationships it was this: pretending wouldn't fix anything.

'Can I ask a question?' Sasha said.

He did wonder then if there was anything he wouldn't tell her. 'Go for it.'

'Do you choose not to drive or is it not an option?'

'I could if I really wanted. Hand controls would be safest, but I like public transport. The more people use it, the better it gets—better for everyone.'

'I looked at the bus option to get to the stadium tonight and just gave up, got a taxi.'

'It's simpler than it looks.' And then he offered to show her, because they were going the same way home. No third drink. No throwing caution to the wind. Okay, so this might be a first date, but Cam was determined not to do anything reckless. There might be a second date, but there wouldn't be anything M-rated happening tonight.

Outside, they paused, waiting for traffic. Neither one pressed the button to trigger the lights, but there was a decent gap.

'You good?' she asked, stepping out to cross.

'I can jaywalk with the best of them,' he said.

'Jaywheel?'

He smiled, pretending he hadn't heard that one before.

'I'm trying not to make assumptions.'

'I appreciate that.'

'Or ask nosy, intrusive questions just because I'm a curious medical nerd.'

'Surely you know me well enough to know that,

if you ask something I don't want to tell you, I'll say so.'

'Yeah, but that doesn't mean I want to be that person.'

'You have my permission. Ask. What do you want to know?'

She took a moment to consider, then said, 'Does walking hurt?'

'Not *hurt* hurt, but it's like a stretch. It burns. I tire quickly, and not in a predictable way, some days faster than others. I used to walk more, which you'd think would mean it got easier, but the difference was minimal.'

'You mentioned that Neroli taught you to walk. Just big sister being big sister or…?'

'Oh, kind of.' He didn't want to make Sasha feel sorry for him. Didn't want anything from this woman out of pity—and he wanted quite a lot, if he was honest. But when she didn't ask another question, he kept talking. 'The doctors told Mum I wouldn't be able to walk. She believed them, because why wouldn't she? They're the experts, and she had a lot on her plate, two little kids, work, and our dad was totally useless—did us all a favour when he finally left. Sometimes giving up is the best option.'

'But Neroli didn't give up?'

'Neroli wanted someone to play with. I don't really remember it, to be honest. I was maybe four. I remember falling down on pillows in the hallway. I remember dancing, hanging onto the side of the sofa. I remember chairs spread out across the room, every few steps, so I had something to grab onto. And it worked enough—gave Mum enough hope that she got on board and convinced the physios.'

'Is that why you became an advocate?'

'Maybe. It's why I became a physio.'

They were coming up to the bus stop, and she didn't say anything else until they were on the bus. Instead of taking the empty seat only a row back from the wheelchair bay, she stood, one hand above her head, holding onto the railing. As though she wanted to be close to him. As though she had more to say, more questions to ask. Maybe he should just tell her no, no more questions. He felt as if he'd said too much and not enough. He felt as if she could see right into his soul.

'There aren't many physios who use wheelchairs,' she said.

'Yeah, no kidding.'

'Not many doctors either,' she said.

He shook his head.

The bus swung around a corner, but she was steady on her feet. She had on a blazer over her tee shirt, black with bright pink stitching and gleaming gold buttons. It matched the pink laces and yellow stitching on her boots.

'What is it?' she asked—probably because he was staring at her feet.

'Nice shoes,' he said.

She pulled up the ankle of her jeans to reveal a chunky gold heel. These were bold shoes, sexy as hell, probably expensive. 'I like 'em,' she said, as if talking about her favourite cookies, not a pair of boots that likely cost more than his whole outfit. But what did Cam know about the price of fancy shoes anyway? He was warring with himself. This wasn't about shoes. This was about wanting what he couldn't, or shouldn't, have.

She leaned back on the pole behind her. 'They don't hurt at all the first couple of hours, but then it starts with this low-key awareness that your feet aren't happy, you know? Like it's there, but it's not serious. Then, maybe half an hour later, you consider taking them off for a bit, just for a break.'

'You can if you want,' he offered. 'Borrow my shoes. They've barely touched the ground.'

She gave him a bright smile, almost a laugh. 'Nah, if I take these puppies off, I can't put them back on again for weeks. Gotta wait till you forget the pain. You know, how you forget pain.'

'Yeah, I'm familiar with the concept.'

'Anyway, it's not so bad. I wasn't on my feet that much this evening. It's not even at the daggers bit yet.'

'The daggers bit?'

'There's a point when every step hurts like walking on blades, and you feel the bruises in your bones—here, and here.' She lifted her knee, cocking her leg to point to her foot.

The bus hit a pothole or something. She grabbed on and maybe she was fine but Cam grabbed her foot, held it against the armrest of his wheelchair. 'Brace yourself,' he joked.

'Maybe I should sit down.'

He met her gaze, pretty sure she could read his mind, though he didn't ask aloud, *sit right here, on my lap?*

Her smile now was crooked, all mischief and temptation and *nice try* and *maybe I will, then.* But she was too smart for that. Too sensible. She swung around the pole and sat on the nearest chair. 'It does feel good to take a weight off.'

'I bet.'

He happened to notice out of the window. 'Shoot, that was our stop.' He pressed the button, but they were past it now.

Sasha said, 'What's a bet these shoes go dagger mode the minute we step off this bus.'

'How far to your place?' he asked.

'Couple of blocks.' She didn't stand up until the bus came to a complete stop. 'Thank you,' she said to the driver, stepping off onto the kerb, the gold on her shoes glinting in the street light.

It took a moment for the driver to set the ramp in place. Cam had to smile, watching Sasha wait for him, standing on one foot, then the other, flexing her feet. 'Dagger mode?' he asked as the bus pulled away.

'Not yet.' She started walking back towards their usual stop.

They'd go past his street before then, but he might not mention that. He'd see her home safe.

'Don't get me wrong, I'll definitely be happy to take them off.' She meant her shoes, not anything else. Best he wasn't thinking about anything else. But her hips were at his eye level, right there in his periphery. Not that there was much to see in this light, and her blazer covered plenty, but his imagination filled the gaps. What if she was wearing *only* those boots?

'Well, if you want to be carried, just say the word,' he said. Apparently his brain was no longer in full control of his faculties. This was bad. This was not the plan.

'You want me to sit on your lap?' Good, she was calling him on his nonsense. She was smart and sensible and making good choices.

'I won't pretend I won't enjoy it,' his runaway mouth said.

'Did you enjoy it last time?' She gave a laugh, as if she'd surprised herself.

'Finally, an invasive question,' he said.

'I don't know what's got into me tonight.'

They passed his street and kept going, the silence easy between them.

She sat down at the bus stop when they reached it. 'I just need a moment.'

'You should take them off,' he said.

'There could be broken glass.' She flexed her feet, stood up again and swore. 'What am I trying to prove? You really don't mind?'

'Mind what?'

'If I hitch a ride?'

'Not at all.'

Oh.

This was really happening.

'I need to see the path, so sit sideways,' he instructed.

She stood in front of him, clearly unsure how to approach this, so he took charge, tugging her hand till she sat down, all her weight on one of his thighs. The tight muscle almost liked the pressure, but it would hurt before long.

'Legs up,' he said, but only dared touch below her knee. He wasn't about to manhandle her. She got the message, hooking her knees over the armrest. 'You can hold onto the seat back,' he suggested, because he wasn't ready to tell her how to touch him. Not yet.

Not yet? The thought was right there, eager, impatient, and far too confident.

As soon as he pushed the wheels forward, they hit a crack in the pavement and she slipped, the curve of her backside notching between his thighs. That was more comfortable, the pressure more even, but her hip was brushing rather close to… yep. Okay, think about unsexy things. Think about the path ahead of them. Think about avoiding potholes and loose gravel and anything else that could send her flying. Think about the burn in his arms, not the heat of her body grazing against him like some kind of cruel dream, close, so close, but not actually touching.

Then all of a sudden it was touching, not because

she'd moved, but because he was a mere mortal and he wasn't made of ice.

'So, what number is your place?' he asked, a meagre distraction tactic.

'Thirty-one. It's my sister's place.'

'Right, of course.'

There was a tension in her body. She must have noticed—he was hard against her, no use denying it, but she said, 'So, what should I be looking out for at these apartments I'm viewing tomorrow?'

'Um…' Think, Cam. Brain, function. 'Doorways with lips. Narrow spaces, especially tight corners. High light switches and door handles.'

'You could come with me. I'll pay your consulting fee in bougie brunch?'

The pavement was rough for a patch, and they slowed to a stop.

She turned her head to face him, and she was right there, close enough he could hear her breathing. Soft orange street light caught on her lips, her cheek, her temple, but the rest of her face was shadows. She moved closer, that was the clue, and that was enough. He was done wondering. He wanted this. She wanted this—well, she wanted something.

Hell, she could have whatever she wanted.

That first kiss glanced off her lower lip, as though they were both asking permission. But the next one was all answers. He raked his hand into her hair and held her there, taking her willing mouth. Taking this reckless moment in the dark. They'd have to work together. They'd have to act professional. Act as if he didn't know how her breasts felt pressed to his chest. Act as if he hadn't tasted her mouth. As if she hadn't curled her cool hands behind his neck and rolled her hip into his erection.

The blissful pressure tore a groan from his throat.

The sound, there in that quiet street, dragged Cam back to reality.

They weren't going inside together. They weren't going to bed together. This was a goodnight kiss.

CHAPTER SEVEN

SASHA TORE HERSELF AWAY, clambering off his lap. Her lips tingled. Her whole body, in fact. 'I can walk from here,' she said, tugging her clothes straight.

'Sasha,' he said. It wasn't the first time he'd said her name, but it seemed strangely significant. She'd been Dr McBride, a surgeon, an ally one moment, adversary the next. But now she was definitely Sasha. Melting at his touch and moaning into his kiss.

She felt so young in that moment. There was something about standing on the street, late at night, the awkwardness of it, the rush of heat and want and hunger, so out of control, catching her by surprise.

A laugh slipped out of her.

Then he was laughing too. It was a good sound, his laugh—rich and light at once, like a crackling fireplace. It made her want to kiss him again.

Instead, she kept walking towards her sister's house. 'It's the blue gate there.'

He nodded. 'Email me the apartment listing.'

She wasn't going to kiss him goodbye. She'd already kissed him goodbye. Although it hadn't felt like goodbye. It had felt like a taste, teasing at her appetite, waking up her senses. It had felt like the beginning of a feast, a dégustation menu, numerous courses, each surprising and satisfying and leading on to the next.

But the next course would have to wait. 'Goodnight,' she said. 'Thanks for the ride.'

He laughed. 'My pleasure. Obviously. Sorry about that, by the way.'

'You don't need to apologise.'

'Still, it wasn't…intended.'

'No?'

He cocked his head to the side and that look, as if he was having downright filthy thoughts about her, made her clench in all the right places.

'Sleep well,' he said, wheeled around, and rolled away.

Inside, Sasha saw her sister's coat hung up on the hook, but all the lights were off. Sasha tugged off her boots and then sent Cam the link to the first apartment listing.

He must still be on his way home—nearby enough that they shared a bus stop, but she didn't know his actual address.

She thought about having a shower, but didn't quite trust herself right now. Her lips were swollen, her body charged. Stripping off, the warm water—she knew what she wanted, but he'd message her back, and then what?

Buzz. New message—he'd used the chat function rather than reply via email: Is that the 9.30am one?

That's the one, she replied. Did you make it home okay?

Almost there. I'm driving one-handed.

Is that safe?

After years of practice, sure, he answered.

And when it seemed as though neither of them had anything else to say, she sent him the next listing she planned to see tomorrow.

Rather than watching and waiting for an answer, she brushed her teeth and changed into her PJ shorts and a worn-thin Chicago Bulls hoodie.

Cam's message was sitting waiting for her when she returned to her bed. That's a whole different vibe, he'd written.

I like the high ceilings, she explained.

Me too, but the heating bills...the message trailed off. Another followed...are probably less of a concern for a surgeon. Never mind.

She was tempted to say something cheeky about creative ways to stay warm. Instead, she asked about carpets and sliding doors.

When she woke up, even before she opened her eyes, the memory of the previous evening sent a rush of heat to her core. Her nipples pricked hard against the thin fabric of her hoodie. Maybe today there'd be a round two.

She opened her messages—there was a new one there waiting for her.

Morning Sasha, I've woken up with a wicked sore throat. Hopefully, I haven't given you a cold, but I'd better not risk it. If you want my take on the accessibility stuff, feel free to send me photos as you go.

Disappointment churned under her ribs, seeming to suck all the air from her lungs. He was unwell and didn't want to spread a virus—as a medical professional she should applaud his choice. As a woman, she wanted to declare the ship had sailed when he'd kissed her last night. And if she was going to get sick anyway, she might as well see him. Touch him. Maybe taste him.

A new message arrived from the property manager confirming her appointment.

And then the dulcet tones of her sister's online yoga instructor filtered through from the living room. Sasha needed her own place, but visiting apartments had just got much less exciting.

In Cam's line of work, everyone seemed to agree on one thing and one thing only: if you were sick, you should stay home. No one wanted your germs. Almost everyone was either immune-compromised or working in an understaffed environment. They all knew not to take good health for granted. So a head cold meant three days of guilt-free laziness, and this time of year, with the days getting shorter, he'd usually be glad of it.

Instead, he was livid. How very dare a boring, run-of-the-mill cold virus—more irritation than illness, the sandfly of infectious illnesses—not only keep him from brunch and apartment-browsing with Sasha, but from two days of overlapping patients on the ward and an advocacy appointment to boot. Rather than cementing their not-just-friendship, he'd been reduced to messages discussing architecture.

Well, she had sent one photo that wasn't a too-narrow doorway or poky bathroom. She'd taken his recommendation for brunch—the barista was a friend of his. Sasha had sent him a selfie with the barista, her latte art in the foreground. The message read, Even better than the hospital cafeteria.

Hopefully she hadn't said that to the barista—it would not be received as a compliment. Cam wouldn't put it past her though. She often did say exactly what she was thinking.

Cam had replied with a photo of his home-made lemon and honey drink.

Later that day, she'd asked for his address and left a paper bag in his letterbox—a piece of ginger root and a handwritten note: Put a couple of thin slices in your hot lemon honey. Get well soon.

She wasn't calling him *honey*, but it did make him wonder if she ever would.

The next time Cam saw her, she was doing rounds on the ward—not with the same patient as him, not at the same moment, but he caught her eye down the corridor, and he came into one room just as she left it. Passing her in that doorway, he caught her scent and remembered the pressure of her sitting in his lap, the tickle of her hair against his chin, the taste of her kiss.

Ahem.

He had a patient to talk to, paperwork to catch up on, and she had places to be.

'How are you doing, Gemma?' He rolled up to the bedside, announcing his presence.

Gemma looked up from her e-reader. 'Oh, Cam, hi. I'm all right. Sore but not more than…apparently it's normal.'

He made a mental note to check that she was getting appropriate pain relief. 'Good book?'

She nodded. 'Historical, a bit gory. Makes me appreciate modern medicine. Back in the day, I'd have been bedridden and probably doped up on laudanum till I overdosed,' she said.

'I would have been institutionalised.' He offered a grimace. 'So, you will have seen the other physios while I was away. Have you been up and walking?'

'Yep. Gah.'

'What?'

'I keep unintentionally nodding my head.'

'It won't do any damage. Don't worry.'

'Just feels wrong.'

'Easy does it. Can you flex your feet for me?' She did, back and forth, probably the same exercises the other physio had started her with each day, getting her ready to walk. As he moved through the series, he asked about her recovery more generally. He wasn't going to bring up the robotic assistance, but he was curious if she was still thinking about it.

'I just want to go home,' she said. 'It's hard to sleep here. There's always people coming and going.'

He directed her to slowly stand up.

'Dr, um, Bride…?'

'McBride?'

'Yeah, her, she said the robotic thing meant I'd be able to get out of here faster, but I don't know what faster is—faster than what?'

'Okay, well, I'll see what I can find out.' It was the perfect excuse to speak with the surgeon. 'You would have had a follow-up with her yesterday or the day before?'

Gemma nodded. 'Yeah, she says it went really well, and the other surgeon too—maybe the boss or some higher-up?'

'Vivian Stirling?'

'That's the one.'

'She's Head of Orthopaedics.'

'Fancy robots *and* fancy humans. Anyway, all worth it if I can go home sooner rather than later.'

'I'm glad to hear you're happy with how it all went in the end.'

'They've got to come up with a better name for this robot thing, eh?' she said. 'I'm picturing a dalek with needle-arms and radioactive eyes.'

'Wow, I may have nightmares about that.'

'Why are daleks so scary? It doesn't make any sense—pepper grinders wielding egg beaters. But they really are.'

'Did you see the new episode?' he asked and let

Doctor Who carry the conversation while Gemma walked the whole length of the corridor. Eventually they talked meds and pain levels, and Cam typed notes into his phone while she got back into bed.

He went to find Sasha.

No sign of her, so he asked at the nurses' station.

'She has surgery in an hour, so she can't have gone far.'

He went down to the surgical suites and found her coming out of Pre-op. 'There you are,' he said.

Her face lit up. That right there, *that* was the kind of response he wanted every time he saw her. 'Thanks for the ginger,' he said.

She looked around, as if they were guilty of something, as if they had an avid audience. She nodded down the hall and he followed her into a small room, empty but for a reclining chair and a couple of magazines on a small table—all set up for waiting around before surgery.

Sasha closed the door. Surely stolen moments in private rooms were the quickest way to start rumours. But Cam felt bold, nervous, excited all at once.

She said, 'You can't just casually announce I'm dealing in ginger root. That's the kind of homoeopathic remedy that'll tank a doctor's reputation around here.'

He laughed. 'An illicit root? Yeah, that'll do it.'

She shook her head, trying not to laugh, but that smile shone in her eyes. 'I'm glad you're better.'

'It was just a cold.'

'Back at it?'

'Still catching up. I was just with Gemma Edie. She had a couple of questions about meds, but mainly wants to go home as soon as she can.'

Sasha nodded. 'Another couple of days at most, all going well.'

'Best-case scenario?'

'Tomorrow, maybe.'

'Brilliant.' He ran through another half-dozen quick questions.

Sasha perched on the edge of the armchair and answered them all, fast and clear.

In the tiny room, they were close together, only a couple of inches between their knees. Cam kept glancing at her mouth. He had to work really hard not to be distracted, to hear only her answers and not the warm timbre of her voice, a little sigh, the hum of agreement as if it might be something else. He typed her words into his notes, hoping he hadn't missed anything.

'Do you suspect she's in more pain than she's let on?' There was care in Sasha's voice, gentle concern; nothing alarmist, just genuine interest.

'I don't know. She said her pain levels were *apparently normal*—it made me wonder where she's getting the *apparently* from. I just wanted to check.'

'We can go see her. I have some time now.' She looked him right in the eye. The awareness between them kicked up a notch—or maybe it was all in his imagination—but he was suddenly very aware, from the soles of his feet to the top of his head and everywhere in between, that they were all alone and she was right there. She had some time now. He leaned a little forward in his chair; it wasn't even a conscious decision, just his body reacting to her proximity, and his thoughts were probably written all over his face.

She rocked closer for a moment, too, then pulled away, cleared her throat. 'These rooms have cameras, just in case someone reacts to a sedative or…'

'Right.'

'I have surgery at two, but we could catch up after.'

'Yeah?'

'It's another robotic-assisted procedure. Plastics are keen to see it in action. The precision appeals for microsurgeries and things like targeted muscle reinnervation.'

'Is that for amputees' phantom pain?'

'Yeah, we talked about it with Joshua Tait—our first patient together. Not for him, but then adding in a robot doesn't make it an easier sell—as you've pointed out.'

'Blame science fiction movies.'

She cocked her head to the side as if physically struck by an idea. 'How are you with blood?'

'What? Why?'

She laughed. 'Don't worry, I just thought you might want to watch a surgery—see it for yourself. I should warn you, though: if you're expecting sci-fi, it will probably disappoint. Coolest piece of tech

I've ever worked with, but we are still within the realms of, you know, reality.'

'I can watch?'

'If you want.'

Did he want to watch her? Um, absolutely. Performing surgery. Or doing really anything else. 'Okay, then.'

Sasha was being observed by two plastic surgeons and a surprise late arrival from Cardiology, but she was more nervous about Cam. Why did she want to impress him? And why, of all things, was she attempting to do it by removing damaged cartilage from the medial compartment?

Surgery was, thankfully, useful for more than osteoarthritis—it was also a pretty effective focus-grab. When she was in the zone, nothing and no one else existed.

When she came out of the zone, job done, she was met with questions and introductions, requests and stories and bids for collaboration.

The operation was a success. But it was also a good twenty minutes before she got away from her colleagues. Cam had probably given up waiting. Who did she think she was? Bold to assume he'd waited for her at all. As if she was some kind of superstar? She'd done her job today, no more and no less.

This was the comedown, a not at all unfamiliar post-surgery funk. She could explain it chemically, but that didn't make her immune.

So when she saw him chatting with the clerical staff down the hall, she felt it like a physical rush. He had waited. He hadn't left. She went from low to high in one dizzying moment. Oh dear. She had it bad. But damn, it felt good.

He was several metres away, not even looking at her let alone touching her, and it was like the sun coming out after three days of rain. One human person should not be able to shift her mood so dramatically without even realising he was doing it.

This was bad.

And then he spotted her and smiled. This was good.

He gave the clerical staff a distracted nod farewell, then wheeled his chair towards Sasha. She had his full attention, and the look on his face was quite something. The smile was gone; in its place an earnest, eager, perceptive interest. He was really looking at her. As though he wanted to know everything.

'What can I say?' He gave a shrug, shook his head. 'That was incredible.'

'What was?' she asked.

'The surgery.'

'Oh, right.'

'Just an ordinary day in the office for you.'

'Well, kind of—that is my job.'

'Still. Is it weird that I've never watched one before?'

'Not really.'

'It feels weird, given how many knee-replacement patients I work with. All the before and after bits, but never when they're actually…'

'Unconscious?'

He cocked his head to the side. 'Just take the compliment.'

'Compliment taken.'

'That was amazing,' he reiterated.

'It went well,' she agreed.

'The robotic-assistant thing wasn't as… *Blade Runner* as I was expecting.'

'I haven't seen *Blade Runner*, but I'm guessing that's a good thing.'

'Evil androids,' he said.

'Not a lot of those in the OR.'

'Just the surgeons,' he said, smile cheeky as all heck.

She laughed, even though she probably shouldn't. Those android-ish surgeons were the colleagues she needed to make a good impression on. That'd be easier if she liked them. Which would be easier if she weren't laughing at their robotic tendencies.

'Wait, am I included in that?'

'No.'

'Are you sure? I can be rather abrupt.'

'You lack the cold metal.'

'And nerves of steel,' she said, but he was right: there was nothing cold about her just now. He had her all warm and willing and he hadn't even touched her.

'The thing is,' he said, as if he had bad news and hadn't found the words, 'calling it a robotic assistant is always going to play on people's minds—no matter how un-robotic the surgeon. But I have an idea.'

'I'm all ears.'

'We should work together.'

'We already work together.'

'On rebranding the robot.' He was serious. He wanted to help, and he was the perfect person to do it. 'On how to explain it to patients so they know what they're in for but they aren't freaking out.'

'That's the dream,' she said, but looking at Cam in that moment, she believed it—the dream could be reality.

'Let's do it.' He grinned.

She could have kissed him. Instead, she checked the time. 'I need to pop into Recovery in like half an hour.'

'Yeah?'

'Strike while the iron's hot? We can go to my office, or do you want to see the robot up close?'

'The robot?' His eyes lit up with mischief, pupils wider by the moment. It was all unsaid, but how could she doubt it—he wanted to see *her* up close. 'I'm guessing I'm not allowed in the OR.'

'It's being cleaned. The robotics are kept in here.' She led the way, swiping her lanyard over a keypad to open the door.

'Touch-free,' he said. 'Does that mean we're not allowed to touch anything?'

'Everything gets resterilised before it's used.' She walked in ahead of him. 'You can touch whatever you like so long as you're…' She realised what she'd said, but it was too late to unsay it, so she continued, ‘So long as you’re gentle.’

‘I can be gentle.’ He looked like the cat who got the cream. ‘So,’ he said, a shameless pivot, ‘point me at this robot.’

She took the covers off and pointed out a bunch of features, moving parts and data ports. ‘We upload the pre-op CAT scan and basically do the whole operation before the actual operation, but it’s like a simulated version. If that makes sense.’

‘Like a video game? What are the pin things that go into the bone?’

‘The arrays. Like mini satellite dishes, they basically map out the surgical field and line up the computer model with the real thing.’

‘So you plan out exactly what you’ll do on a virtual version of the patient’s anatomy? But based on their actual body.’

‘Yeah, it’s all patient-specific.’

‘And the actual things that do the cutting, the…’

‘The instruments?’

‘You still operate those.’

‘Yeah, I guide the instruments. Does that make it less scary?’

He nodded. ‘So what does the robot do during surgery?’

‘It shows me the live image—without me having to crane my neck or cut the joint wide open to see it.’

‘So it’s a communication thing. The robot’s not performing the surgery at all.’

'No, it's an assistant.'

'But so are the people standing beside you in the operating theatre, so…'

'I suppose this assistant involves several moving parts and some of them go inside the human body, so…'

'Sounds like a party,' he said, and then looked abashed. 'Sorry.' He wasn't looking at the robotic assistant now. He was looking at Sasha. 'It's not just me, right?'

'No,' she said, although not much of a voice actually came out.

'I want to take you out for dinner and then kiss you again and not wait a whole week to see you after,' he said all in a rush. Then after a beat, added, 'But we need to work together.'

'Yeah.'

'This is important.' He nodded to the robot.

'It is.'

'Okay.' His tone of voice made it almost a question, the slightest lift at the end. 'I would usually steer clear of seeing anyone from work.'

'Sounds wise,' she said, but wished the words back. She didn't want to talk him out of this.

He let his hand drop into the space between them, elbow on the armrest of his chair, fingertips near enough to reach out and touch the leg of her scrubs. 'If it doesn't work out, we'll still have to see a lot of each other.'

She was holding her breath without meaning to, waiting for contact that didn't come. She didn't want to think about Liam right now, about leaving her job and everything behind when the relationship ended—it had seemed the only option. But Cam was nothing like Liam.

He wheeled his chair a fraction closer. 'We can be grown-ups about this.'

'Definitely.'

'Yeah?' His eyes were intent, like a man begging for bad news.

'What's the worst that can happen?' she said, like a fool, because all of a sudden all of the worst things flooded into her mind.

And apparently into his, too, because he started saying them out loud: 'You suddenly realise there's, ah, some added complexity being with a disabled guy and dump me.'

Well, she hoped she wasn't that flaky. 'You start to find my brutal honesty a real downer.'

'You see right through my hopeful optimism.'

'You realise I'm somehow both too much and, at the same time, not enough?'

'Bull shit.'

'Verbatim,' she said, and here she was living up to those very words, being way too honest and having nowhere near enough self-preservation.

'Whoever he was, he was an idiot,' Cam said.

'I'm not fun.'

'We had fun already,' Cam said. 'Fun is easy. It's the one thing I'm good at.'

'I don't know about the *one thing*,' she said, and resisted the urge to list everything he was good at because that was a bit too much like writing love poems out loud.

And she didn't *love* him. Where had that come from? She *liked* him. Liking was…fine. Liking was harmless. He deserved to be liked. And not just because he was fun.

'Actually, the worst thing that can happen,' he started, the back of his hand grazing up her leg, 'is getting us both fired.'

She had the vague sense that he'd been meaning to say something else entirely, something more likely, more real. But getting fired, that was genuinely unlikely. 'Not gonna happen.'

'Even if I do this?' He pulled her down to sit in his lap, and before she'd caught her breath, he grazed his thumb across her lips like a warning.

It wasn't the first time he'd kissed her, and the first time had been way more than one kiss. And the gesture that preceded this kiss was far from subtle. Nevertheless, when he captured her mouth, the smooth heat of it delivered a full-body shock. She gasped into it, and then her mouth was open, and that was probably the best decision-that-wasn't-even-a-decision of her life. Cam's tongue did wicked things, curling into hers, the gentle tug of suction, the hum of a moan—was that him or her?—vibrating low and deep, and then all that slick warmth, smooth as caramel and sexy as sin.

This wasn't a kiss, it was a seduction.

And then he swore, right into her mouth, as if she

was doing the same brutal, brilliant number on his body as he was on hers.

'Yeah,' she agreed.

He looked her right in the eye, his pupils blown wide and dark. So she kissed him again; it was only fair.

It was too easy. She fitted there on his lap as though she belonged and grabbed onto him as if she was at risk of tumbling onto the floor. Her scrubs were thin, her heat unreal.

'No patient-observation cameras in here,' she said, and then kissed him again.

'Good to know,' he murmured into her mouth, and his hand was on her thigh so she didn't fall off his lap, but now he was super aware of it—the soft-and-firm-at-once feel of her body beneath the cotton. He felt her muscle tighten and release, and it made him think of other muscles contracting and relaxing.

Her fingertips were dipping inside the collar of his shirt, cool against the fever rush of wanting her.

'The getting-fired odds are higher if I take this off,' she said, 'aren't they?' She meant his shirt. She wanted to take off his clothes. 'But I can still reach a little.' Her nails were grazing between his buttons, his nipples pricking hard at the almost-touch.

'Clothes on seems wise.' He spread his fingers wide on her thigh, inching towards her hip.

'General rule for the workplace,' she agreed.

'Hmm,' he said, because words seemed harder

by the moment. The waistband of her scrubs was rough beneath his fingertips, but it didn't give when he tugged at it.

She smiled into the kiss and stopped touching him—wait? Why? But the answer was she was lifting her scrubs top and tugging at the tie beneath. Just like that, he could slip his fingers inside her clothes, feel the soft skin of her hip, the crease at the top of her thigh.

'This okay?' he asked, teasing at the hem of her underwear.

Her answer wasn't a word, but a sound, neck arching, pressing her breast to his chin.

'Was that a please?' He kissed her throat, tasting the salt on her skin. Her pulse beat steady against his lips, his tongue.

'Please.' Her voice was just a murmur above a whisper, rough and breathy.

He gave her underwear a tug and earned a sound like a sob. He had to know, had to touch her and know for sure how wet she was. 'And this?' The warmth of her felt like home beneath his hand. She was pressing up into his touch.

'Don't stop,' she said.

Cam gave her underwear another tug, aiming to tease, but she moved into his touch; inviting it. The irresistible silk of her coaxed him to explore. This was already more than he'd intended. 'Are you sure?' he asked.

Was *he* sure, though? Parts of him were, yes, absolutely, one hundred per cent. But he'd been here before. Well, not *here* here. Not when anyone might walk into this not actually locked storage room at any moment. Not risking infamy in every hall of this gossip factory disguised as a medical facility.

But here in the sense that he had, more than once before, stumbled into the start of a capital-R relationship that could leave him wrecked. Sasha had a strong sense of right and wrong. She was a good person, a determined person, with good intentions…the kind of person who might, on some level, date a disabled guy and keep on dating a disabled guy, just to keep up with her own moral compass.

The way Sasha gave way against his touch, the way she pressed up, tightening against his hand—this right now seemed like pretty solid proof she was legitimately into him.

She was fumbling with the button of his fly. And for reasons passing understanding, that shocked him. He didn't want to do that here. He wanted to feel her quiver, coming apart around his fingers. He wanted to fix her clothes and send her off into the hallway flushed and tousled.

He wanted to keep something back for next time. Because there was going to be a next time.

But stopping her hand was impossible. There was only one way to distract her now. He caught her swollen core, making her groan and writhe with pleasure.

'Harder,' she begged. Her eyes snapped open, as if surprised by her own self. Then she was looking him right in the eye as she came.

He kissed her—not just to quiet her sounds but because she was quite possibly the most beautiful sight he'd ever laid eyes on. Kissing was the appropriate response to those eyes, lids heavy, and those lips, swollen and gaping and moaning, and that neck, arching in pleasure, and that earlobe, soft and supple between his teeth. She shuddered against him and it was all he could do to keep from bucking into her hip like a dog in heat.

Later. There'd be a later.

There had to be a later.

Sasha's skin was alight with sensation, every pore hyper-sensitised, her nipples pricking hard against the lace of her bra, and her underwear had to be ruined. But when she looked at herself in the mirrored steel on the back of the storage room door, she couldn't see any clues that might give away what they'd been doing in here.

Good God, what had they been doing in here?

'You okay?' Cam said, adjusting himself.

A laugh escaped her lips, more surprise than anything else. He was asking if *she* was okay? She'd just orgasmed harder than she ever had with another human being. 'I'm just fine,' she said. Understatement of the century. 'Are you sure you, ah, don't want…?'

He shook his head. 'I mean, obviously, I very much want, but worth the wait.'

'I need to swing by Recovery, but we can, ah…' Even the thought of a sequel had her greedy body clenching around nothing at all and longing for his touch again—his hands, his mouth, and that deliciously insistent hard-on she'd had pressed to her hip while he was stroking her to ecstasy. 'I can't believe we just did that.'

He grinned, all cheeky and mischievous, and she leaned down to press a kiss to his mouth. 'I'm going to hide out for a little longer in here, if that's okay.' Cam glanced down at the straining fly of his jeans.

She nodded, backing towards the door because she really needed to leave. But still, she was thinking about unzipping him, taking his steel in her hands, tasting him, knowing just how far gone he was. She was thinking about straddling him, lowering herself onto the thick length and begging him for every inch.

Oh, this was bad. 'I'd better go,' she said, before she did something reckless. Something *more* reckless than riding her colleague's fingers, grinding into him while he kissed her neck.

She stepped out into the hallway, touching her fingers to her throat and hoping he hadn't left a mark there. She picked up her white coat en route and put the collar up. Perhaps it would look accidental and cover any evidence.

It was nearly an hour later before she got to a bathroom to check in a proper mirror. No telltale pink bruises, thank goodness, but there was a silly look on her face—*that* was surely suspicious. She massaged her cheeks, as if she could rub the smile off.

Oh, this was bad. This was the kind of lovesick nonsense that made people suckers. Then she saw she had a message from him. Oh, thank goodness. Maybe if they could just finish what they'd started, she would be able to rein it in at work. She shouldn't be so desperate. It was too much too soon, all this longing and impatience and neediness.

She splashed water on her face and made herself wait before reading his message. Her phone sat on the counter beside the sink, taunting her with her own unruly response to his name on her screen.

But Cam's message was about work—he had a patient for her to consider. Is it you or Plastics you'd recommend for three years post-amputation. He's using this prosthetic but has a lot of phantom pain. There was a link to the prosthetic model.

She replied in the same vein. I'll talk to Plastics and see what they think. The willpower it took to resist every urge to invite him to dinner. Or skip dinner and drag him straight to bed.

But her bed, the one in her sister's spare bedroom, was *so* not ideal—not for seducing a man who could certainly make her loud. And Cam had said it was *worth the wait*, so hopefully he'd invite her to his place…at some point.

She walked back out into the ward, hoping work would distract her from her own impatience. Ten minutes later she was in a helicopter with Neroli and two paramedics, en route to the port. 'Two guys are trapped in the space between the shipping containers, one with his arm stuck, the other says he's fine, but we couldn't get at them when we first arrived, so we took the head injury and left the ambos to do what they can.'

'When you say his arm is stuck…?' Sasha said into her headset. The pounding rhythm of the blades just above her was making it hard to speak in complete sentences.

'Is it crushed or are we thinking severed?' asked Neroli, who was clearly more comfortable in a helicopter.

'We couldn't get near enough to see.' The paramedic answered Neroli's—and Sasha's—question. 'They're clearing the way as we speak.'

Neroli turned to Sasha. 'Did you do emergency call-outs at your last job?'

'Not often.'

'Don't worry. I got your back.'

The helicopter roared loud, gaining altitude as they approached the hills.

'Cam said you're moving house,' Neroli said, as if the sudden ascent wasn't surprising her at all. 'I moved recently, so I have boxes if you need some.'

'Thanks, but everything's in transit.'

'Which part of town will you be living in?'

'Central, near the park.'

'With an elevator?' Neroli asked, and if that wasn't code for something… The question was what? Cam had told his sister something. What exactly that something was…

They were cresting the top of the hills, the view opening up below. 'Wow, it really looks like a volcanic crater from this angle,' Sasha said, craning to see the port.

'Wait, we're not landing on a boat, are we?' Neroli asked the pilot.

Sasha felt her adrenaline spike at the thought.

'No, thankfully we're on dry land. Dry-ish. There was some petrol spillage—not a lot, but enough we need to be careful.'

Their descent was steep enough to kill all conversation at that point, but the radio was busy with the voices of air traffic control and the pilot, and the sound of the helicopter itself picked up again. Sasha closed her eyes and took a slow breath in through her nose. Hold. Slowly out.

Neroli's hand was warm on her arm. Sasha opened her eyes and met the steady gaze. Maybe it didn't matter what Neroli knew, exactly. It'd be nice to think that Cam would tell his sister about anything or anyone important in his life—it was nice to think Sasha might be one of those things. Sasha had fobbed off her own sister's curiosity about the basketball date, saying only, 'It was fun.' But Sasha's sister wasn't one to push a confidence, whereas Neroli would probably go right ahead—it was strangely endearing.

The ground greeted them with a gentle thud, and the engine cut away almost immediately—clearly they weren't taking off again in a hurry.

Outside, the incident manager directed them through a labyrinth of shipping containers. 'We've got one of them out,' he said. 'He's in the ambulance now, looks okay. But the other guy's arm is really wedged in.'

'Is he conscious?' Neroli asked.

'He was when we arrived, was talking and yelling, but he passed out before the paramedics got access.'

'Vitals?'

Sasha listened, stepping around dark puddles on the ground. The first she saw of her patient was a silver emergency blanket rippling in the breeze and catching the light.

'The fire-and-rescue team are all set up to move the container.' The incident manager stayed back while Neroli and Sasha crouched down beside the paramedics. 'But it'll swing a little when they do, so we need everyone out of the way.'

The man's arm was pinned by the edge of the fallen container, disappearing from sight just below the elbow. His sleeve had been cut away, the ratty edge of the fabric hiding the worst of it.

'I'm gonna need to intubate him,' Neroli was saying—the implied question being, *am I doing that here or after we move him?*

'How long has he been trapped?' Sasha asked.

'Twenty-five, maybe thirty minutes.'

Sasha turned to the incident manager. 'If he's lying here when you lift the container off, is he in range of it swinging?'

'Possible.'

Neroli handed the paramedic a bag of isotonic saline. 'Even still, he might arrest from reperfusion, and we can't help him if we're standing at a safe distance.'

She was right. This was why Sasha was here. Sure, she'd rather be doing this in a sterile OR with three specialist nurses, an assisting resident and an anaesthetist, but that wasn't an option right now.

'I'll amputate here,' Sasha said.

CHAPTER EIGHT

CAM HAD BEEN accused of being an optimist more than once. It bugged people—usually people whose physical capabilities were all tied up in their identity, their sense of worth and purpose—it offended them that a guy in a wheelchair might be happy and secure and confident.

It wasn't that Cam didn't have low moments, didn't doubt himself or experience immense frustration; he did. But he saw a lot of hope, too. He had front-row tickets to the miracles of modern medicine. If someone was on the orthopaedics ward, generally they'd just undergone the most major surgery of their lives. Their pre-surgery pain was fresh in their minds, arthritic joints grinding like broken glass, and Cam got to spend his days watching them take their first steps pain-free.

Mrs Turei was glowing, smile wide, eyes bright and teary. When she finished their first walk—just a few steps across her room—she lay back on her bed and cried with relief and joy, clasping his hand. 'I can visit my *moko*.' *Moko*, short for *mokopuna*—

her grandchildren. 'They live in an upstairs flat, and I couldn't get up the stairs.'

'We'll have you going up and down stairs before you leave hospital,' Cam assured her.

'Really? That soon.'

He nodded.

'I want to say something—is the doctor lady here? Blondie. The surgeon. Is she around?'

'I can find out.'

Cam found Sasha with another patient, heard her voice behind a curtain, and waited. Cam knew the patient—Willy Barker, double knee replacement. He was a city councilman, gregarious and opinionated and hard not to like.

'They want to get me some big, ugly chair for my desk,' Mr Barker said with a laugh. 'I told 'em I'll just use one of the waiting room chairs. They're solid and all right angles, uncomfortable as sin but there's one with armrests.'

'Sounds workable,' Sasha said. 'You'll need to take regular breaks, walk around, keep your knees from getting stiff. But that's at least four weeks away yet, you understand. Four weeks minimum.'

'Yeah, got it, and I'll ditch the walker by then, eh?'

'Perhaps.'

'When I get an idea in my head…' Mr Barker gave a cheeky laugh, then turned serious. 'I don't want people making a fuss.'

'I understand that, and applaud your determination, but long-term recovery rests on short-term rehabilitation. Taking risks in the near future can cost you. I get that you don't want to be a nuisance, but—'

'Oh, I don't mind being a pain in the arse. Just ask the mayor!' More laughter.

'The workplace accommodations are there if you need them, that's what matters.'

'But if I do all this physio and tick the boxes for the next couple of weeks, I won't need them—and that's best for everyone. That's what I'm all about, making things better for everyone.'

'Are you trying to get my vote, Mr Barker?'

Cam noticed the curtain moving. They were wrapping up. He had the sudden urge to hide.

What had he sought her out for? His head was full of what he'd overheard. Mr Barker's perspective wasn't exactly unusual. Able-bodied people prided themselves on being 'low maintenance'. But Sasha had simply accepted his statement about making things better for everyone. *Everyone.*

She pulled back the curtain and smiled when she saw him. 'Cam. I mean Mr McColl. Are you here for Mr Barker?'

'No, we had our session earlier.'

Mr Barker pointed one finger gun at Cam. 'I'll be doing these exercises three, maybe four times a day. This city ain't gonna run itself.'

Sasha walked out into the corridor alongside Cam. 'He's certainly motivated,' she said with amusement in her voice. 'What did you need me for?'

Right. Why was he looking for her? 'Oh, it's Mrs Turei. I think she just wants to thank you.'

'Miriama Turei, yes, she's third on my list now. Tell her twenty minutes?'

He nodded.

'Something else?'

Now was not the right time. She had a whole list of patients to see, and so did he, to be fair. He'd say what needed to be said, just later. 'It can wait.'

'Okay.' Her phone buzzed and she checked it. 'Sorry. My sister is trying to help me buy some furniture and she keeps sending me pictures and links.' She pulled a face at her phone. 'We have somewhat different taste.' She showed him a photo of a plain white bookcase, nothing remarkable about it. 'I like a bit more character,' Sasha said. 'Anyway, better get on.'

One of the things Sasha liked about her job was the variety. Surgery was a challenge in a completely different way from ward rounds. Outpatient appointments were different again. The intense, high-stakes focus and precision required in the OR were one kind of exhausting. This was another: making just enough small talk to get on with the real reason she was there.

She wasn't the only surgeon who preferred the surgery bit. The controlled environment, everyone an expert, doing their part, no interruptions, total focus. Not that surgery always went to plan, but, more often than not, she could run to time. The same could not be said of ward rounds. It didn't help that she was curious what Cam had to say, and she was getting her hopes up, and trying not to get her hopes up, because that was where danger lay.

Her phone buzzed—probably another soulless side table her sister had found online. Thankfully, after tomorrow, Sasha had a couple of days off; she'd found a thrifting blog about all the antique and second-hand stores in the city. She'd already picked out a new bed and arranged delivery. Just over a week till moving day!

The text wasn't from her sister, however. It was Cam: I have a break coming up—slim chance but thought I'd ask.

She scanned her appointments, checked the time, checked the list again. Who was she kidding? As if she were going to turn him down. But she liked the idea that she would—she could turn him down if she needed to—the idea that she retained that much control over her own self.

Fortunately, her schedule today didn't put that theory to the test.

I can take five now or after my next patient.

He was in the staff break room when she got there. Lockers lined one wall and there were showers next door, fresh scrubs stacked up here, ready to go—and Cam, shirtless, standing up to reach the tops.

'Want a hand?' she asked.

'I got it.' He pulled on a shirt and she watched, without really meaning to.

When she realised what she was doing, noticing the mole on his side and the ridges of abdominal muscle, the dark hairs on his chest and lighter on his stomach, she turned away and asked, 'What happened?'

'Mr Henry managed to knock his whole water jug onto me.'

'Water, well, that's best-case scenario around here, isn't it?'

'Exactly.' He sat back in his wheelchair and swivelled to face her. 'Do we actually have a break at the same time?'

She shrugged. 'I made it work.'

His smile made her melt. She *was* getting her hopes up here, no denying it, but the look on his face, all hope and a bit of surprise, as if maybe this wasn't quite what he'd expected, as if he was nervous, too. As if maybe they were on the same page.

She filled up the kettle, ignoring another buzz from her phone.

'More bland furniture?' he asked.

'Probably.'

'I have a big old bookshelf cabinet antique I was thinking of selling,' he said.

She leaned back on the counter, waiting for the water to boil. 'It's okay. I've got a list of antique stores, and until I'm moved in there's nowhere to store anything, so no real hurry.'

'When Neroli and Sorin got together, I moved

into her old place, and she left most of her furniture behind. It's more than I need, and it gets in the way of my chair—tight corners and narrow spaces aren't ideal.'

'Oh, right. Well, I could take a look.'

'I can send you a photo.'

The kettle got louder, seeming to shush their conversation. 'Tea? Coffee?'

'Tea, please,' he said and went to the fridge for the milk. 'Hey, so I overheard your conversation with our local councilman earlier.'

'Mr Barker. He's a bit of a character.'

'Undeniable.'

'I don't know if I'd vote for him, but you have to admire his dedication. Thinks he'll be back in the office in a month.'

'In an office without accommodations.'

'He doesn't want anyone making a fuss.'

'It is a common way of thinking. But the idea that everyone is better off if people don't get the accommodations they need…? *Everyone* is not better off. Anyone who does need accommodations is the exact opposite of better off.'

'I think he meant that he was hoping not to *need* the accommodations by then. He's motivated by the prospect of getting along without them.'

Cam nodded, clearly unsatisfied by this.

She waited, hoping he'd say what he wanted to say, what he needed to say and what she, perhaps, needed to hear. She squeezed the teabag with a spoon, the clink of metal against the mug the only sound in the break room.

'I've had a fair few accommodations in my time,' Cam said. 'And I've had to fight for them. And plenty of people don't or can't fight that fight—I get that, it's a lot, and we all choose our battles. I wouldn't blame any disabled person for choosing *not* to fight that fight. But it concerns me that we're applauding people who can get on without accommodations. The more people who use them, the more common and available they are, the less fighting required.'

Sasha took a seat at the table. She hadn't thought about it like that, but many of her patients did have to fight that fight. She should have realised. She knew all about choosing her battles—she was a woman in medicine—but accommodations were outside her personal experience. And that was the problem: her understanding shouldn't be limited to her personal experience. Not in this job.

'Thanks,' Cam said, taking his tea.

'I didn't think about it like that.'

'I know.'

'Did I *applaud* him? I don't remember what I said.'

'Nothing that he hadn't said himself—we don't need to unpick the whole thing; no good comes of that. But he works at the council. Hundreds of people share that workplace, not to mention their influence over the public spaces in this city. Having disabled folks in places like that can be a game-changer, but the chances of us getting those jobs, staying in those jobs, aren't great.'

'He has a follow-up in a couple of weeks.' Maybe she could say something to him then, encourage him not to push himself, highlight the risks, and reassure him about using accommodations—make him understand the upside not only for his own rehabilitation but for others. 'He says he wants to make the city a better place. Maybe I can convince him that playing it safe with his rehab does double duty of… Okay.'

He smiled again, a proper smile, the kind that made her gooey, made her feel privileged to be on the receiving end. Silly, to tell the truth, because he smiled like that at everyone. His warmth and positivity and generosity seemed boundless, touching everyone he met—she wasn't special, not really. But the feeling wouldn't be turned off by logic. He smiled, and Sasha felt *chosen*.

Cam's last stop of the day was a new advocacy case. It was an odd one from beginning to end. The man was already in hospital, whereas first appointments usually took place in Outpatients. The application was half empty, but that wasn't uncommon. Removing access barriers meant they kept the required fields to an absolute minimum. The information didn't really add up, though. Three days post-operative was early to be applying for Disability Advocacy Services, unless this had been a planned amputation—but the notes said it was a workplace accident, a crush injury. Perhaps the patient had a close family member who was disabled, someone who was helping them navigate their new reality.

He scanned down to the declaration at the bottom. This application hadn't been made by the patient. Sasha McBride had filled this in. Maybe he should talk to her in person before proceeding, but when he asked at Reception they told him she was in a meeting with Dr Stirling and half the hospital execs.

Cam opened up the man's medical notes, instead. Oh, this was the emergency call-out with Neroli, the accident at the port—they'd both mentioned it to him. He'd brushed Neroli off because she'd obviously been fishing for an update on his relationship status. And Sasha...well, he'd got distracted in other ways.

There was nothing for it. Cam went into Mr Clarke's room and found the man staring out of the window. He didn't hear Cam enter, but that was partly due to the wheelchair—no footstep sounds.

'Mr Clarke,' Cam said. 'Good afternoon.'

From the jerk of his shoulders, clearly the man had been miles away. He gave a sharp inhale—perhaps pain, perhaps just annoyance. Cam had spent enough time in hospitals to know what it was like on the ward: constant interruptions when you didn't want them and no one to be found when you did.

'My name is Cameron McColl. I'm with Disability Advocacy Services.'

'What?' The look on Mr Clarke's face—he wasn't even looking at Cam. He saw only the chair.

'We offer a range of services. We can, ah, go along to appointments and help with bookings and transport, make sure you have all the information and…' Shit. This guy had clearly never heard of Disability Advocacy Services. This guy had lost almost half his arm just days ago and wasn't ready to hear the word *disability* out loud, let alone own it. And seeing Cam's wheelchair was a slap in the face. A wheelchair—the universal symbol of disability. 'Excuse me,' Cam said, but before he could turn around and wheel his disabled arse out of there, Sasha arrived.

'Oh, good, you're here. I wasn't sure I'd done the application correctly.'

'Yeah, we should talk about that.'

'Not to worry, we're all here now. Mr Clarke, how are you feeling this afternoon?'

Mr Clarke stuttered the start of maybe an honest answer and maybe something sharper.

'Can we speak outside?' Cam asked.

Sasha's enthusiasm cracked. 'Ah, okay. Be right back, Mr Clarke.'

Cam spun on the spot and followed her out into the corridor. 'Did Mr Clarke request a disability advocate?'

'Well, no, I just thought you'd be better able to explain what you do than I could, and he's been through a lot—it's a big transition, so I thought you could sit in and help him through it.'

'But he didn't ask for an advocate.'

'I asked him if he'd like someone to help him with decisions and understanding what was happening, and he seemed open to it.'

'Seemed open to it is not the same as agreeing,' he snapped, then bit back the rest of what he wanted to say. She hadn't done this on purpose. It was a careless mistake, in part an ignorant mistake.

A well-intentioned mistake.

One that might come at quite the cost to Mr Clarke's recovery. The look on the man's face—the look on Sasha's face right now, all confusion, as if nothing he was doing or saying made a jot of sense.

'When someone is going through such a big transition, as you put it, they need, more than ever, to feel in control of their care. Add to that, I show up…' He gestured down at his wheelchair. 'Not the best way to tell someone they're disabled now.'

She paled. 'Oh. I didn't realise.'

'I know.'

'I'll fix this,' Sasha said. 'How do I fix this?'

Excellent question, and he had no answer. 'Just leave it. He needs time,' Cam said, and he needed a moment himself. The way Mr Clarke had looked at Cam, at his chair, a mix of horror and disgust, confusion and fear; it'd take a minute to shake that off. Thank God it was the end of Cam's shift. He could go home. No, he could go to the gym. Lifting would make him feel not just strong but in control. Sure, it was something of an illusion, because he was so very far from in control—of Mr Clarke's reaction to his chair, of the man's recovery, of really any of his patient's opinions of him, of his own emotional response to the whole palaver, never mind his feelings towards Sasha McBride. But he had to do something with all this—so weights it was.

CHAPTER NINE

IT WAS LIKE that feeling when you didn't realise there was a step and your foot went down on thin air. Then the ground dropped away and you lurched off balance, stumbling to find your footing. Except recovering from a missed step was the work of a minute, tops. Sasha had come home, joined her sister and niece on the sofa watching some English quiz-meets-comedy show, pretended everything was fine…but it was not fine. The way Cam had said, 'He needs time.' 'He' was Mr Clarke, but she had a feeling Cam might need time, too. She'd messed up. She'd rushed ahead, overconfident and certain she knew best. She'd got an idea in her head and hadn't really listened to her patient. Again.

She drafted and redrafted a text to Cam, but every version seemed to ask more of him. Her apologies would corner him into offering reassurances. If she tried to explain, to understand, to fix things, he'd only end up doing unpaid labour, teaching her about all her ableist blind spots, her arrogance, her tunnel vision.

Above her blinking cursor, three little dots appeared. Oh God, he'd been watching her stop and start writing this message. And then his message arrived—no endless back-and-forth necessary to word this perfectly: he'd sent her a photo of a bookshelf. A floor-to-ceiling, real wood, beautiful piece of furniture.

It's perfect, she typed and hit send, quick, before she could second-guess another word.

He replied within seconds: I just clonked my funny bone on it. Again. Perfect is not the word I called it.

Hope you're okay! But honestly, name your price.

You might want to measure and check it'll fit, he replied, and she realised he would probably refuse to let her pay him. She'd find a way, though. And for starters, a selection of pastries from a local bakery that perpetually had a line out of the door.

She'd stopped thinking about her mistake.

'Sasha,' her sister said.

'Yeah?'

Her niece laughed.

Sasha shoved her phone aside as if she'd been caught. 'What?'

'We both said your name like five times.'

'Is it basketball-game guy?' her sister kicked off the interrogation.

'No! It's a bookshelf.'

They both grinned, shaking their heads—mother

and daughter matching gestures and idiosyncrasies like a choreographed dance—as if they didn't believe her at all.

Cam held the metal end of the measuring tape in place and passed the roll to Sasha. She was at his house, and they both had the day off, and it all felt a bit too good to be true.

'It's kind of perfect,' she said—she meant the bookcase. 'I can put my old photo albums in the bottom—Mum will be glad to offload those, and the crystal my grandmother left me.' She wrote the measurement in her notebook.

Cam gestured which length to do next, and she understood without a word—another green flag, alongside their shared taste in furniture.

He wasn't unconscious of the not-so-green flags, but it was so much easier to ignore them when new green flags kept popping up. She'd said all the right things when he'd pointed out the flaw in Mr Barker's logic—couldn't have asked for a better response. What had happened with Mr Clarke still hurt, but that was a genuine mistake, a procedural error more than anything else. Cam was only feeling it because of Mr Clarke's reaction to *him*. It was personal. Cam couldn't be objective, couldn't trust his feelings on this.

He'd thrashed himself at the gym last night, adding another callus to his left hand. But it *had* helped, had thrown off the panic, the fear, the ghosts of relationships past whispering in his ear about history repeating.

And then he'd come home and sent her photos of the bookcase.

Which the universe was rewarding him for, apparently: Sasha had arrived on a warm breeze with *pain au chocolat* and cheesecake-stuffed doughnuts. There was something about seeing her in genuinely casual clothes: hair down, a little windswept; a frayed denim skirt; bare feet in slides, and a loose sweater, off the shoulder. It was one of those mid-autumn days when summer came back in full force for one last hurrah.

Sasha reached up on her tiptoes to hook the end of the tape measure over the top of the shelves. He leaned forward in his chair, bending the tape against the base of the furniture and only glancing at her bare legs for the briefest of moments. He read the measurement aloud, but the scent of her erased his short-term memory entirely.

She wrote down the numbers and said, 'Now I just need to find a sofa, and a small dining set, and maybe bedside tables.'

'You can check the measurements. You don't have to decide here and now,' he said.

'It'll fit somewhere.' She tapped her notebook. 'These measurements will help me figure out where and how. It's actually so perfect. There's something about bare wood. Warms the place up.'

He wasn't going to say anything, but the thought

was there—bare wood, the idea of warming her up, of being bare.

She must have seen it on his face because she laughed. 'I mean furniture. But sure. That too. I'll shut up now.'

'I don't want you to shut up.'

'No?'

He shook his head. 'Tell me something.' He was asking for more green flags, for distraction, anything to keep him from thinking about Mr Clarke's look of disgust, and the way Sasha had said, *he seemed open to it*, and *I...applaud your determination*, and *I didn't think about it like that*...and it was hardly the first time he'd had to explain something that, to his mind, didn't take a heap of imagination to figure out. But able-bodied people rarely used their imaginations to do that kind of figuring out. Even able-bodied people who were in a close relationship with a person with a disability. Every dating experience of his life warned him not to expect it, and yet he kept on hoping it wasn't too much to ask.

'Okay,' she said, 'I'll tell you something: when things are going well, I'm waiting for the other shoe to drop.'

'When things are going well? You mean at work?'

'I mean, yeah, at work, there's this funding we might get, Vivian Stirling is positive, and she's a great boss, but I keep expecting something to blow it all up in our faces. And other things are going well, too. I found an apartment. With an elevator.' She cocked her head to the side, met his gaze. 'Made a few friends. Maybe more?'

'Only maybe?'

That earned a laugh, a light shove to his shoulder. He didn't have the brake on, so the chair moved back a little. He grabbed her hand to draw closer again. But then he was holding her hand, and he couldn't help marvel at it: at what surgeons' hands could do, but more than that. Her skin was soft, her grip tender but strong. His own hands were calloused, dotted with freckles and often grazed or bruised, between basketball and bumping into door frames and furniture. Sasha's hands, though—he pressed his lips to her knuckles. She smelled like pastry, like butter and sugar, utterly satisfying.

Oh, but satisfied he was *not*. That little taste of her had his appetite roaring with want.

She gave a soft gasp, so he did it again, following the space between her fingers, kissing, then licking.

She swore. Then laughed. Then said, 'We could…'

'We could,' he agreed.

'Finish the house tour,' she said, a cheeky smile, a blatant tease.

He nodded, playing along. 'Spare bed is there. Do you want to see the laundry room?'

'If that's what you want to show me.'

'Not a lot of rustic furniture there, so…'

'No?'

He was leading the way to the master bedroom. He was in the high ninety per cents sure that was what she was meaning. 'You'll like the old-fashioned dresser, the bare wood.' He paused at the doorway, pivoted to see her face.

'Very nice,' she said, peering into the room.

'The drawers?'

She laughed. 'The bed, too.'

'Go ahead,' he said, and in she went. She ran her hand across the front of the dresser drawers and then went to the bed head. 'Is this rimu?'

Cam nodded.

'I'm no expert in New Zealand trees, but it's a hard wood, right?'

'I think so. You'd want a hard wood for a bed.' Thank God he'd done his full set of stretches after his workout.

'Generally speaking.' She cupped her hand over the ornamental bit on the end, which suddenly looked blatantly phallic—how had he never noticed before? 'May I?' she asked.

'I have no idea what you're asking, but yeah, you can do whatever you...'

She sat down on the edge of his bed, which put her eyes at the same height as his, and she looked right at him. 'What do you want?' she asked.

'I'd have thought that was obvious.' And getting more obvious by the moment—just watching her had him swelling and stiff in his jeans.

'Come here,' she said, and he saw that she was nervous. He didn't want her nervous. He wanted her to tell him exactly what she wanted. He wanted her to ride his hand again, to ride *him*, to hold onto that rimu headboard and test just how sturdy the hardwood was. He wheeled the chair forward till their knees touched. She parted her thighs, pulling him closer, his knee between hers. The heat of her body burned straight through his jeans. She threaded her fingers through his and kissed his knuckles, just as he'd done to hers minutes ago. 'I want to know,' she said.

'What do you want to know?'

'What you like.'

'I like you.'

'What works for you.'

He laughed a little because this was working for him, this gentle teasing, this gentle touching. But he knew what she was asking. 'My arms are strong, my legs not so much. I'm more flexible mentally than physically,' he said, and gave into the temptation to touch her bare shoulder. 'I'm game. What works for me is figuring out what works for you.' He leaned forward till he could press a kiss to that shoulder, inhale her scent at the junction of her neck.

'That's nice,' she said on a sigh.

He tongued at her pulse and she lifted her chin, offering her throat.

'But it goes both ways,' she said, her voice shaky.

'Sounds good to me.'

'I mean, knowing it's working for you, that works for me, too.'

'Oh.' Now that was quite the thought—that she was turned on by his arousal. That the sight and sound of his pleasure was getting her off.

She tugged him closer, till his kneecap was

seated in the apex of her thighs. And her knee was just grazing at his erection, trapped painfully behind a zip. The button on his boxers was leaving an impression.

'A little discomfort,' he said, thoughts zigzagging through the blood rush. 'Might make this last longer.'

'I don't want to hurt you.'

'Well, okay.'

'You'll say?'

'I'll say.'

She kissed him, her mouth barely open, a tentative invitation. How could she doubt he wanted this? But that was a conversation for later. Right now, he'd kiss every doubt away.

Sasha let the kiss take her, pull her under. Coming up for air was overrated. Kissing this man was better than air, better than anything. And the pressure of his knee between her thighs was nudging her dangerously close to the brink. She wanted to buck her hips, wanted to make him just as wild for it.

But sitting like this, there was so little contact between their bodies. She was barely touching him. 'Can we lie down?' she murmured half into his mouth.

He nodded, and kept on kissing her as if it were a lifeline. As if there was no hurry. The urgency in her blood was the best kind, and resisting its pull only upped the ante. She traced her fingers down his neck and inside his collar.

He laughed and swore as if this was just as overwhelming and surprising to him as it was to her. 'Go on,' he said, nodding towards the bed, and while she scooted back, kicking off her shoes, he stood up. She lay there in the middle of his bed and watched him lift his shirt up over his head, let her eyes linger on every detail—the dark hair high on his chest, the pattern of it across his pecs, pale brown nipples, a few freckles, lines of muscle, all drawing her gaze down. The waistband of his underwear sat just an inch higher than the top of his jeans. And there was no ignoring his arousal, straining at the zip.

He fingered the button above and she looked up, held eye contact, nodded, and watched his already dark pupils blow full wide. When he joined her on the bed, he was down to only his underwear, and there she was, still fully clothed. But he didn't seem in any hurry to even things out, leaning over her, resuming kissing, ignoring the occasional graze of his erection on her hip, pressing, a little more insistent, against her belly. Her blood was roaring, wet heat pooling, wanting pressure, wanting him. She rolled her hips, trapping his steel between their bodies, and he groaned, broke the kiss, breath stuttering.

Good. That was where she wanted him, because that was where she was—*so* far gone. She ran her hands up his body, nudged him to lie down. But he grabbed her hips, kept her close. And then his hands were up inside her sweater, thumbs pressing the underwire of her bra. A moment later the clasp gave; it was strapless, nothing to stop it falling away. His hands were warm and rough on her breasts. He drew a fingernail across one nipple and she didn't even recognise the sound that ripped from her throat. He chuckled, the vibration of it rumbling through his body and into her bones.

She sat up enough to tear off her sweater, and the cheeky look fell right off his face. She was kneeling, straddling his thigh, and his expression was all the encouragement she needed to press her need into the hard plane of his thigh.

He sat up in a flash, palming her breasts with hungry hands and then following with his mouth.

The first time she touched him was an accident, the backs of her fingers grazing the tented fabric of his boxers. When she did it again, he twitched to meet her touch, and when she bared him, moisture was beading on the smooth head, coating her palm.

He sucked in a breath, and her nipple was in his mouth, so she felt it—the rush of cool air, the graze of his teeth, the throb deep inside, begging for more.

'We can do this like this,' he said, sliding his hand up the inside of her thigh where she was desperate for contact. 'But if you want to change it up, there are condoms in the drawer just there.'

'What do you want?' she asked.

'I'm enjoying your hands, in case that wasn't obvious.' He looked her in the eye, his fingertips teasing at the lacy edge of her underwear. She nodded permission, and he pushed the fabric aside. He'd touched her there before, but not like this, not with her legs spread and breasts bare, glistening where he'd licked and kissed. He curled a finger in the slick heat, then another. 'I have calluses on my hands. If it hurts, just say.'

She could only whimper as he traced the lines of her body. When he touched her, her legs almost gave. 'The headboard is out of reach,' she said, almost laughing, almost. Her body was too charged, every touch intense, every nerve hungry.

'Can't have that,' he said, and moved backwards till he was right up against the pillows. He pulled his underwear free and sat there waiting for her.

She got up, stripped away the last of her clothes, and tossed him the condoms. 'Just in case,' she said, and crawled up the bed. She kissed his legs, watched goosebumps rise on his skin, grazed her breasts up his thighs.

'Oh my God,' he whispered. So she pressed her open mouth to his steel, tasted salt and breathed in the musk of want, of need. He ran his hands through her hair and tugged her up to face him, to kiss him, and she was so aware of the taste of him on her tongue, now on his. This was so intimate, *so* much. She felt as if she might cry, the emotion of it thick in her chest.

Then his hand was on her hip, guiding her closer. His touch was so gentle, as if he was tracing the shape of her, learning his way by feel, testing a stroke, a tap, a squeeze, a tight circle. And then she was coming with a rush against his fingers and crying out. And he was watching, gaze rushing up and down her body, making eye contact as if to say, I see you. I see *all* of you.

'I want you inside me,' she said, and heard how demanding she sounded, how needy and shameless.

'I am inside you.' He curled his fingers and she clenched around them. And that was nice—better than nice, but still, she reached for the condoms.

He laughed. 'Okay, let me.'

She watched him slide one on, followed his hands with her own, felt his desire throbbing beneath. 'Okay?' she asked.

He nodded, lifting her leg so she straddled him, sliding him against her. 'You feel so good. I could have come just touching you.'

She rose up, notching him further down, and let the anticipation build for a beat. And another. And when she gave in, pivoting forward to take him, she was already coming again.

Cam slid home in one stroke. He saw stars and moaned, but it disappeared into her sounds. She rocked, taking him deeper, her body gripping his, the liquid heat of her enveloping him. The way they were together, he wanted to make this last as long as possible. So he held her there, let her take her pleasure, but didn't let her pull back, because that'd push him over the edge.

The rush of sensation settled, just a little, and she opened her eyes. 'I wasn't expecting that,' she said, voice hoarse—from the scream of her orgasm. 'Sorry, I think I blacked out there a moment.'

'Never apologise for coming on me,' he said, and reached between them. 'In fact, I want you to do it again.' He rolled her sensitive nub between his fingers and she laughed. The shudder of it went straight through him. He was deep inside her, in the luxurious heat of her willing body, but he drew his focus, used every bit of willpower. He laved at her nipple, drew it to a tight nub, tasted the sweat on her skin and felt her shiver. But by some miracle he didn't lose it.

'Am I allowed to move now?' she said. 'I have to move.'

'Please, God, move,' he said, and hardly recognised his own voice as she rose up. The rush of cool air felt like nothing else, and she drove down onto him and swore, and did it again. As though she couldn't get enough, every inhibition slipping away. He took control, every other part of him in service—hands gripping her hips, muscles tight. Oh, he was so close now. He should touch her again, bring her there with him. But he couldn't stop what he was doing. And then she was arching back and crying out. She was right there, and so was he—it wasn't a choice now, tumbling over the precipice together. He was shaking, crying out, and that final rush, when it came, threw his whole body into the most divine release.

She fell forward onto his chest, pinning him down, and he felt as though he'd have lifted right off the bed otherwise. Levitated. Exploded in a burst of colour and light.

'Oh my God,' she said on a sigh.

'Did I die?' he asked.

'Three times, and that last one counts for more than one surely. Cam. What?'

He laughed. 'What *what*?'

She shook her head and looked him in the eye.

He straightened to kiss her, and that shifted the angle between them. He should deal with the condom. This was risky, staying like this afterwards, but he couldn't bear to break away when every gentle touch was like magic. It had never been like this, not with anyone, and he wasn't counting orgasms—it was the way they fitted, the way they moved together, the way she met his gaze and held it, the way she said what she wanted, and clung to him, strong and tender at once, the way she laughed and then turned serious, the way she gave her attention, her touch, her whole body.

He was falling in love with her.

This was why they called it falling: nothing he could do about it, no way to slow the pace of it, no amount of flapping his arms—the laws of physics could not be denied. And he gloried in his helplessness. He could do nothing but feel the rush, enjoy the view, try not to think about the landing…

Falling was the right word, yeah. But the tense was misleading, as if this were just starting now, in progress. It'd be more accurate to say he had fallen. Not that he was going to say so, not yet, but the truth remained: he was in love with Sasha McBride.

CHAPTER TEN

SASHA TOWELLED HER hair dry and walked out of the bathroom. Cam wasn't where she'd left him in his bed. Rumpled bedding and a crushed box of condoms spoke to the desperate things they'd done there earlier. Her body was still humming. She'd never come that hard before, never mind three times.

There was music on somewhere else in the house. She followed the sound and found Cam putting something into the oven.

'Hope it's okay; I borrowed this.' She flicked the tie of his robe, which she'd found on the back of his bedroom door. Putting on her clothes again seemed too much, too final. She didn't want this to be over.

He looked her up and down. 'It's never looked better.'

'What are you making?'

'Shakshuka.'

'Oh my God, I think I just came again,' she joked and took a seat at the kitchen table.

He rolled over, nudging one knee between her

thighs, and just before he kissed her said, 'These are a few of my favourite things.'

'Eggs and a spicy tomato sauce?'

'And the way you come.'

'How long does that need to bake?' She ran her hand up his thigh and under the hem of his boxers.

'Long enough I could do an appetiser. Sit up on the table for me.'

'You don't have to…' she started to say, but the look in his eye was all desire. He wanted this: wanted her to spread her thighs, wanted to trail breathy kisses up from the inside of her knees until he was lapping at her still swollen clit. The rough stubble on his jaw. The rhythm of his tongue. The way he moaned, as if he was enjoying this as much as she was. Her body had never responded like this before, but in minutes she was bucking into his mouth.

Robe falling wide open, she slid off the table and into his lap. They'd left the condoms in the bedroom, which just now seemed too far away, so she took him in her hands, kissing his mouth, and moving against him until he gasped and went rigid and spilled over her fingers.

They cleaned up and ate outside on the sunny front porch. Cam joined her on the sinky, sun-bleached sofa, their legs tangled between them. She was dressed now. And hungry. And her mind was going ninety miles an hour. They'd gone from a tentative almost-date to the most intimate connection of her life, and the weird bit was that it didn't feel too fast at all. But it should—she was smarter than this. She was sensible. Realistic. Logical.

She took a forkful of runny yolk and spicy tomato and looked over at him.

He raised his eyebrows in question—he wasn't asking if she liked the food; she'd already said it was delicious.

She said, 'Why doesn't this feel ridiculously fast?'

He only cocked his head to the side, a thoughtful look on his face. 'Maybe because we've already had a few bumps in the road.'

'Maybe.' That could be it—their first fight, and almost a second one, over and done before their first kiss. 'And we work together, so there's some trust…'

'Speaking of working together, I'm excited to start on rebranding your robotic assistant—is rebrand the right word?'

She nodded. 'Me too. And the timing couldn't be better; we need more patients on board. There's a sizeable funding round we might qualify for if we're across departments.'

'Yeah? What's the funding for?'

'The robotic assistants—different departments have different needs, and if there's good uptake we'll be fighting over the one piece of tech, so it makes sense to get more if we can.' Saying it aloud was something else; Sasha hadn't dared to hope, when she moved home, that it would go this well, this quickly. 'It's nice to feel like I can have a positive impact, you know? Well, of course, *you* know. You're always helping people.'

'Surely every operation is helping someone.'

'Yeah, but beyond my immediate reach, people I never even meet. The hospitals I worked at in the US were so much bigger, and the old boys' club was so tight, so set in stone. I worked hard, but it never felt like it really made a difference. Here, it's been so much easier to find a place where I can…' Belong? That was what she wanted to say, but it felt presumptuous because she was sitting on his sofa, eating his food, and she didn't really mean belong *here* here. But she wanted to. 'Vivian Stirling is a big part of it,' she said instead; that was safer. 'Having a woman for a boss—it shouldn't make a difference, but it does.'

'Of course it does,' he said.

Just like that, he got it? He was too good to be true. The fragrant shakshuka, the gentle heat of his legs tangled with hers, the dappled sunlight and autumn leaves—this was *all* too good to be true. So she changed the subject: 'So, robot-rebranding thoughts? Where do we start? WALL-E and what's her name?'

'EVE.'

'I'm impressed.'

He grinned. 'The whole Pixar collection was my go-to when I used to babysit Jules.'

'And now?'

'We play a lot of *NBA Street* on the PlayStation

2, which is miraculously still working even though I got it when I was his age.'

'I love it when things last a long time.'

'Like chunky wooden bookshelves?'

'Exactly. And sinky sofas.'

'Getting up out of this one is the real trick,' he said.

And she managed to stop herself from saying that maybe she wouldn't—she could just stay here forever instead.

Cam sat by the window, the sun on his back, and watched Mr Siems walk the length of the room. 'You're favouring your left leg,' he said, and the man adjusted. Walking would demand complete and total focus for a while yet.

Cam, however, was not *totally* focused. He kept seeing Sasha from a distance, catching a glimpse, hearing the lilt of her voice. She'd been away for a couple of days, moving into her new apartment, and he'd missed her—really, ridiculously, *missed* her. Never mind that he'd still spoken to her every day, gone by with pizza after his shift on moving day, kept up an almost-constant text conversation…

And now she was back at work, his hunger wasn't anything like sated, but just being nearby was enough to keep him flying high—too high, probably, for something this new, but every attempt to rationalise, to bring himself a tad down, out of the stratosphere and into a more sensible altitude, a safer height to fall from…yeah, it was no use. He was in the slipstream, hurtling along, his whole being in mortal danger. But there in the flow, it felt still and calm and safe.

Mr Siems returned to the armchair and Cam made some notes. Sasha came in while he was writing, and, by some miracle of self-control, he didn't look up until he'd finished. 'You're making good progress,' he told Mr Siems.

'Doesn't feel like it,' the man replied.

'Yeah, it can seem like that. But we'll have you ballroom dancing again in no time.'

That earned a smile.

Sasha was talking to another patient at the far end of the ward room, but Cam felt her gaze land on him. Next, he was due two doors down. Passing her on the way out was the closest they'd been all day, and he was so desperate for that little bit of proximity. But as he went by, she glanced over. The look on her face was pure delight. In any other context, he'd be nothing but thrilled, but here, where they worked—thank goodness none of the nurses were in the room at that moment because the blush on her cheeks spoke of every private ecstasy.

He paused in the corridor between patients and sent her a text message: If we keep looking at each other like that, we'll be busted before the day is done.

His next patient, Kim Haley, was almost ready to go home, so they spent most of the session with a walker, doing laps of the hallways. Cam was in earshot of the nurses' station and overheard their conversation.

'Ms Aimes is worried about her scarring and wants Plastics to look at her wound,' one said.

'Dr McBride is in a good mood. Never seen the woman smile so much. If she wants a consult, I'd start there.'

Cam froze, keen not to draw attention to his eavesdropping.

'When I asked her how her weekend was, she said good, *really* good.'

'Didn't she just move house?'

'Maybe she had some…*help*.' That was some innuendo-loaded *help*.

'Dr Pierce asked after her last week; maybe there's something going on between them.'

'Saucy surgeons, eh?' The nurses laughed.

Cam's patient was coming back towards him, a determined look on her face. He should really focus, give Ms Haley his full attention. Hospital gossip was hardly new. And Cam knew they were wrong—nothing to be jealous about. Besides, a little speculation could be a good thing: if people thought Sasha was seeing another surgeon, no one would suspect he was the person… The very idea that she was visibly happier because of *him*, it nudged at those old insecurities, the scars of relationships past. But this was so different—Sasha, the way they connected, it made every other relationship seem like playing pretend, going through the motions. With Sasha, it was real.

Ms Haley went by with her walker. 'What's with the look?' she asked.

'What look?' Cam pivoted his chair to follow her.

'You smiled—does that mean I'm cleared for discharge?'

'Ah, probably.' So it wasn't just Sasha's face giving the game away. 'How's the pain?'

'I can handle it,' Ms Haley said.

'Answer the question. On a scale of one to ten?'

'Four or five.'

When he was all done with Ms Haley, he came back out into the corridor and almost collided with Sasha.

'Hi,' she said, and even that one tiny word seemed to burst with their secret.

'We should talk,' he said, pivoting his chair and putting greater distance between them and the nurses' station.

'What is it?' She sounded worried.

'Nothing serious. I just…here.' He pulled open the sliding door to the family room. A few toys spilled from a basket in the corner and a TV silently played *Meet the Robinsons.*

'Now there's a friendly-looking robot,' Sasha said. 'Is that what it is? Did you have a brainwave about the robotic assistant?'

'Not exactly.'

'What's up?'

He closed the door so they wouldn't be overheard. 'We're going to have to be more careful,' he said.

'Careful? With what?'

'With our faces. The nurses are talking about how happy you look. Every time I see you, it's this full-body-awareness thing, like I could burst out of my skin, but we gotta keep it under wraps.'

Sasha didn't know what she felt. He didn't want people knowing about them? Ouch. But the full-body-awareness bit, the 'bursting out of his skin just looking at her' bit—ditto. Thank God it wasn't just her! Knowing that made her brave enough to ask, 'You don't want people to know?'

'Not yet. I mean, not until we want them to,' he said, voice full of uncertainty. 'And know *what* exactly? It's just not time yet, right?'

He made a good point. Nothing to panic about. 'Fair call. We should probably decide what we're doing before we tell anyone else.'

'Exactly.'

'And there's no hurry to put a label on it or anything.' Even saying the words made her feel slightly sick. She wasn't cut out for casual. She didn't want to share him, didn't want to pretend this was meaningless sex. 'We don't need to make any decisions now.'

He looked her in the eye. There was a tension in his expression, then he said, 'Okay, but call it whatever you like, I'm in. I'm not seeing anyone else. I've no intention of—'

She answered fast: 'Right, okay. Well, me neither.' The rush of relief was visceral.

'But that doesn't mean we're ready to…go public.'

'Yeah, of course.'

He checked the door was shut properly, then took her hand. 'This place is gossipy as all heck. And there's probably a couple of boxes to tick with HR.'

'I'm not your boss, so that should be pretty straightforward, surely.'

He stroked his thumb back and forth across her knuckles. 'I've never dated someone at work.'

'No?' She turned her hand in his and felt the calluses on his palm.

'In my experience, the way things have ended,' he said, and sighed, as if he didn't want to finish the sentence. 'I've never understood people who remain friends with their exes. Let's just say, I'm glad I don't have to work with anyone I used to date.'

She cocked her head to the side, acknowledging the excellent logic of that.

'Have you?' he asked.

'Yeah, but in the US it's a completely different system.' Why was she pretending hospital policy was the only potential hiccup here? Because it was the least terrifying of the options.

'Right,' Cam said, his expression serious—perhaps hatching a plan, perhaps worried, or…

'Are you jealous?' she teased, and lifted his hand to her lips.

He slipped free of her grip and traced his fingertips down her neck, a barely-there touch between her breasts to her stomach, pulling away before her belly button and leaving her body wired. Just that simple touch, a fast, reckless movement. That was all it took.

He cleared his throat. 'I could be a little jealous.' He held her gaze. 'The nurses think you're seeing Dr Pierce.'

'What?'

'So we're probably safe a while yet.'

'I don't love that they're speculating about me at all.'

'It's all the smiling.'

'What? Do I not normally smile?' She gave a sigh, head spinning. Was she really that much of a grump the rest of the time that a good mood was so notable? 'My whole career I'm told to work on my bedside manner, be more friendly, and *now* it's gonna bite me in the arse. Didn't anyone notice you're looking pretty smug and sated?' But as soon as she asked the question, she knew the answer. 'I guess you're always so positive and friendly and warm—the contrast is more pronounced because I'm usually such a grump.'

He laughed. 'I like your grumpy face.'

'Shut up.' She reached for the door, ready to walk out.

He put out an arm to stop her, and it was at hip height so she walked straight into it and held the door closed, enjoying the touch, however brief it must be. Then he said, 'I can sound out HR, without giving away anything specific.'

'If you want to.' She had this terrible feeling that she'd rushed him, asked for too much too soon: a definition, exclusivity. She should have held back a little—been less obvious, less needy.

But the truth was she wanted to touch him, to be near him, to talk to him. She didn't want to hide this, even if keeping it quiet was the smart thing to do.

Doctors hooking up with other doctors wasn't entirely unusual, but this wasn't that. It wasn't a hook-up. And Cam wasn't a doctor. Dating him could absolutely hurt her reputation. It was silly, but there was no point pretending otherwise. Rushing to go public would only make it worse. 'There's no hurry,' she said, a roar of voices in her head. She was too much. She felt too much, wanted too much, too fast. Her own voice was in there, too, trying to be rational and sensible and safe. But there were other voices—Liam, even now when all she felt for Cam really threw that mockery of a relationship into brutal perspective. Even the good times now seemed pale and mediocre.

'I don't know,' Cam said. 'Something about you makes me uncharacteristically impatient.'

Okay, so if she was feeling too much, wanting too much, too fast, it wasn't her alone. The idea that Cam might be there right with her should allay her fears, should quiet those voices. But they only rose, as if she couldn't be sure of this without first fighting it, pushing back against the evidence right in front of her: Cam, his gentle hold on her hip, looking at her as if she was temptation personified.

'Sorry,' he said, and dropped his hand. 'Back to it.'

She was still holding the door firmly closed, and the glass pane of it was cloudy, not truly opaque but no one could see through it. So she leaned down and kissed him. And for a moment, all the voices paused—paused for breath apparently because the moment she walked back out into the ward they resumed a steady rumble debating every feeling.

Cam stayed there a moment to collect himself in the quiet family room. He would talk to HR, then they could…make some decisions? If there was a process to go through, best know about it sooner rather than later. Did he have a gap today? Perhaps he could find a moment between appointments, just a quick, passing inquiry. Nothing more than a hypothetical question. Could he pretend he wasn't already head over heels? He'd better.

He pulled up his schedule and saw he was due over at Outpatients. A casual HR drive-by would have to wait.

Then he saw his first patient's name: Nina Sheffield. He'd gone to school with Nina. She had spina bifida and they were the same age, with similar mobility—or that had been the case at school.

Pre-operative physio, that was what she was in for today. Usually, he'd have gone into the patient notes to find out more, but it felt intrusive with someone he knew; he could just let her tell him in person.

Nina was the same as ever. Her wheelchair was covered in sweary stickers juxtaposed with cartoon characters—Captain Planet, Adventure Time, Marge Simpson—and one that said, 'This dark sense of humour is a load-bearing structure.'

'How about this for a sick twist?' she said, once they'd done the bare minimum of small talk. 'I'll be more mobile if they chop it off.' She gestured a sharp cut towards her right knee.

'Amputation?' he asked.

She nodded, the bravado wavering for a moment. 'I've got a few weeks to get my head around it. I've been trying to talk them into amputating for over a year, but the reality of it… Still, the antibiotics are almost worse than the sores—they better not reschedule. Don't get me wrong, I'm dreading it, but I kind of wish it was over and done with.'

'That's a perfectly normal way to feel about a surgery.'

'Right, so, if I'm ever going to walk again I need to be, like, ripped.'

'It helps.'

She swore. 'You're going to add to my suffering, aren't you?'

'We'll ease into it.'

'At least I've got a physio I can swear at.'

'If it helps, swear away.'

'You know it does.'

After their session, Cam went out to Reception with her. In the corridor, they passed Sasha and Dr Stirling deep in conversation. 'We only need another three or four patients if there's clinical overlap,' Dr Stirling was saying.

'For the funding?'

Vivian nodded. 'Any kind of collaboration across specialties does double duty.'

Cam pulled his focus to the receptionist, directing her when to book Nina in for another appointment, but he couldn't help hearing Sasha's voice. 'Yeah, I spoke to Norris about a TMR case—well, a potential case, but nothing came of it.'

'That'd be perfect,' Stirling said. 'We have, what, two amputee in-patients at the moment and a couple of electives coming up?'

'I'll have a look,' Sasha said, but she glanced towards Cam—did she realise he was hearing all of this?

Vivian marched away and Cam turned back to Nina, saying goodbye as if his mind weren't going a mile a minute. The funding application clearly put pressure on surgeons to prioritise particular types of operations—particular types of patients—to tick a box, or multiple boxes as the case may be. But he wasn't going to jump to conclusions and assume the worst. He could talk to Sasha about it. She'd mentioned it to him before. Their relationship was robust enough to handle a difficult conversation. An honest conversation.

CHAPTER ELEVEN

JOSHUA TAIT HAD AGED; that was the first thing Sasha noticed. Perhaps he was still getting used to his prosthetic. He leaned heavily on a walking stick, as if every step bruised.

'How are you, Mr Tait?'

'Good,' he said, too fast to be believed.

'Are we expecting anyone else?' She looked for Cam, remembering that first day they'd met—well, the second time that day, when he'd shown up supporting Mr Tait and been thoroughly unimpressed by her. It seemed so long ago, but it had only been a month.

'Just me.' Mr Tait hobbled past her, ignored the chair, and perched on the edge of the bed. He rested his prosthetic on his good leg as if that was an ingrained habit now—getting the weight off it.

'Your advocate from last time…?'

'He wasn't available, but I didn't want to reschedule.'

She could see he was in pain—no need to ask why he was so reluctant to delay this appointment. 'You can put it up if you want. I'll be right back.'

She left the door ajar and poked her head in at Reception. 'Where's Cam McColl at the moment?'

'The physio? He's in room five.'

'With a patient?'

'Yeah, and he's got another one waiting.'

Okay, so she probably shouldn't interrupt him. Mr Tait was lying back with his eyes closed when she returned. 'Let's have a look, shall we?'

With a sigh and a nod, he sat up, as if every tiny movement cost enormous effort. She checked the wound and he told her when the pain was better and worse, how it was affecting his work, his sleep, his whole life really. 'It doesn't make any sense,' he said, tears in his eyes. 'My senses are lying to me. My brain or my nerves or whatever it is. There's nothing there to hurt, but it still…'

She looked at his file, asked him about his medications, the side effects and dosages. The diabetes complicated things, but he was doing everything right. 'And the nortriptyline?' she asked.

'It takes the edge off,' he said. 'But you said that from the start—that there's only one thing that actually works for phantom pain.'

'Targeted muscle reinnervation.'

'Surgery, right?'

She nodded. 'Nothing as involved as your last surgery, but yes.'

'I think I need to consider it.'

'Okay. I can explain what's involved, but we'll make an appointment with Plastics as soon as possible. It's a matter of redirecting the nerves, giving them something to do, so they don't keep doing what they're doing at the moment.'

'Driving me crazy?'

'Being in pain takes a lot out of you.'

'How long is the waiting list?'

'I'll have to make a couple of calls but…'

'Just a ballpark?'

It was possible they'd get him in sooner if he was part of the funding application. 'I can let you know within a day or two.'

'Right. Okay. Thank you.'

A knock came at the door just as Mr Tait rose to standing.

'Reception said you were looking for me.' Cam nudged the door open. 'Oh, hi.' He spoke to Mr Tait. 'How's the recovery going?'

'It's been…okay.'

Cam gave an understanding nod, expression sympathetic and concerned. 'Sorry I couldn't get across in time for your appointment. We can set up another one.'

'Dr McBride is booking me in; if you're available, that'd be great.'

'Yeah, I'll make it work,' Cam said, and manoeuvred out of the way so Mr Tait could leave.

Sasha followed him out to say goodbye and returned to her office, where Cam was waiting for her. 'I swear, I didn't even suggest it—he asked.'

'Asked for what?' Cam said, confusion and mild amusement on his gorgeous face. It was all she could do not to kiss him, which she resolved not to do, but she closed the door just in case.

'He wants to consider TMR. The phantom pain is debilitating, and he's getting desperate.'

'Right.'

'He brought it up. I went through all the alternatives.'

'It's okay, Sasha. I believe you.'

'Oh.'

'What's with the tone of surprise?' he asked.

'Well, Mr Tait was pretty adamant last time we saw him.'

'People change their minds.'

'And there's a lot on the line.'

'I thought you were confident TMR was the best option.'

'I mean the funding application I told you about—he's a good candidate.'

'So long as it's what he wants.' Cam reached out and took her hand. 'There's no downside here. How many more patients do you need in this application?'

'Two or three.'

'I've had a couple of ideas for our robotics rebrand.'

'Yeah?'

The quirk of his mouth, the way his smile looked as if it tasted sweet—she was leaning in to kiss him when her phone rang. And the man only chuckled, meanwhile she felt all kinds of frustrated.

She looked at the phone—Vivian Stirling calling. 'I'd better get that.'

'I'd better get back to work,' he said.

She answered the phone, watching him wheel around, the muscles in his arms working.

'We have another candidate,' Vivian said on the phone.

Cam was looking for the glass half full, and he knew it. He didn't want to see red flags and Sasha was doing and saying all the right things. She was aware the case could be a conflict of interest. She was desperate to do the right thing, and far too surprised to find he was on her side. What the hell had that ex-boyfriend put her through? It was as if she'd expected Cam to jump down her throat. Or was that on Cam? He'd been pretty sharp with her, a couple of times.

Vivian Stirling wanted that funding and they were close to getting it—just a few more cross-specialty cases would get them over the line. Cam hadn't done a lot of funding applications, but he knew enough to know there would be a deadline.

And Sasha had been advocating for TMR for as long as he'd known her. So much so that he'd gone and read up on the procedure himself. The precision required for redirecting nerves would no doubt suit robotic-assistant technology. Cam was all for it—in theory.

But in practice, they were looking for patients to suit a procedure, and it should really be the other way around. Patient-centred care. But Cam didn't have time to do the conversation justice right now—he'd been running behind all day. He had a full afternoon in Outpatients: next, a shoulder replacement. Pre-operative physio was tricky. His patients were in pain, so everything he gave them seemed to make things worse. But any gains in strength and flexibility would pay dividends in recovery.

Cam's last patient of the day was lined up for a below-the-knee amputation later in the week. She was diabetic, had already missed a couple of appointments, and Cam half expected a no-show. But Cassie Poole came in on crutches, saying, 'The last time I went to a physio it was because I got into a fight at netball—the goalkeeper thought she was God's gift, she dislocated my shoulder. I didn't do my exercises then, and, I'll be honest with you, I don't love the chances I'll do them now, what with everything.'

Cam tried not to laugh, but it wasn't long till he cracked; the woman was a riot—no nonsense, uncensored, and he didn't have to check her notes to know that more than one doctor had described her as non-compliant. But all that sparky energy, if put to good use, might keep her mobile.

She was, in many ways, Joshua Tait's polar opposite, but they were here for the same reason—diabetic complications resulting in elective below-the-knee amputation.

Cam couldn't help wonder if Cassie Poole might benefit from the reinnervation surgery. He wondered if they could do TMR in the same operation as the amputation itself. One general anaesthetic. One major surgery. The risk, the cost, the stress—all of it halved if she could have the procedure done once and for all. But Cam wasn't a surgeon. He couldn't say anything to Cassie.

He could talk to Sasha, though. They'd planned to work on their robotic-assistant rebrand after finishing for the day. He'd bring it up then.

Not exactly the most romantic location for a date but, oddly, the empty operating theatre felt close and intimate with just the two of them there and only one light on. Even with the robotic assistant for a third wheel.

'There's R2-D2, Optimus Prime and, of course, Bender.' Sasha listed them off on her hands. 'Yes, I googled famous robots, and no, none of them are going to make someone feel better about a robot doing surgery.'

'Not that the robot does the surgery,' he said.

'True.'

'So let's focus on the assistant bit,' Cam suggested. 'A human analogy might be better. One of Doctor Who's companions.'

'Sherlock's Watson,' she counter-offered.

'Samwise Gamgee,' he said.

'"I can't carry it for you, but I can carry you."' She did the accent and everything.

Cam was so gone for this woman.

'What?' she asked, presumably about the sappy, love-struck look on his face.

He scrambled to think of another assistant. 'Goose in *Top Gun*.'

'Doesn't he die?'

'Spoilers,' he said, and that earned a smile, which apparently did something to his brain because, for better or worse, he thought of 'What's-her-face in *The Devil Wears Prada*.'

'Anne Hathaway.'

'Yeah, her.'

'Wouldn't kick her out of bed,' Sasha said.

'I knew you had good taste,' he said. 'Okay, so the robotic assistant's new name is Anne Hathaway, because nobody could possibly object to Anne Hathaway.'

'Working title.'

'Hey, it's progress.' He forcibly turned his attention to the robot, sitting there beside them. He wasn't here to bask in her beauty and attention. He was here to get his head around a real and complex problem. 'So it's a fancy tool, like a smartphone version of a…scalpel.'

'Right. We could compare it to upgrading an old device.'

'People do love an update,' he said. 'They'll line up around the block for the new iPhone, the limited-edition sneakers, the smartwatch.'

'So, keyword: smart.'

'Make it a status symbol. It's not just elite tech.' He was so enjoying the back-and-forth, it hardly mattered what he was saying. Did he really think surgery should be a status symbol? Of course not. And what was more, he was pretty sure Sasha would agree.

She was half laughing, saying, 'It's the superior surgical experience. Treat yo'self.'

'Not just your average operation.'

'Shame it looks like an alien space probe.' She cocked her head to the side.

Cam laughed. 'Now that you mention it.'

Sasha wasn't sure this was helpful. Were they making progress? Impossible to say. But she was having too much fun to really care. It was almost disturbing how much she was enjoying this. The banter, yes, but more than that, the collaboration. The feeling they were a team. She was getting ahead of herself, but it couldn't be helped: what would it be like to go home to this every night?

'Oh, I didn't get around to visiting HR,' he said, interrupting her happy imaginings.

'It was busy today,' she said, more than willing to make excuses, to pretend she was less impatient, less terrified. He had *offered* to sound out HR—it was his idea. But a tiny voice in her head asked if she'd pushed him into it. 'And HR can be daunting,' she added, as if there were no other reason he'd put it off. She was so aware that Cam hadn't done this before. Maybe he'd just been sensible, steering clear of workplace romances, but she suspected there was more going on there—the women he'd dated in the past, the way things had ended, it must have been bad. She couldn't quite bring herself to ask about that, but the only other explanation was unlikely.

'You're not worried about your job, surely,' she said. 'Everyone likes you around here. You're respected on a professional level, but more than that.' She couldn't help envy him a little, the way he was trusted, even admired. Sasha, on the other hand, was an outsider who'd been given enormous responsibility, which some of her colleagues undoubtedly felt she hadn't earned. Her reputation was the one that would take a hit if this thing with Cam blew up in her face. God knew, it was her reputation that had suffered in Chicago.

'You don't have to tell me if you don't want to,' Cam said.

'Tell you what?'

'What happened last time.' He was asking about Liam. Did she really want to open that can of worms? But perhaps if she did, he'd reciprocate, let her see his wounds.

So she said, 'I was one year ahead of Liam, not technically his boss when we first started dating, and it was all on the books with HR before I got promoted. He'd seemed fine with it, but I always wondered if he resented…'

'Your authority?'

She nodded. Liam had *said* he liked 'sleeping with the boss'. In private, he got off on being bad, defiant, enjoyed a little power play—nothing extreme, and it didn't bother her, at least not at first.

At work, they would disagree from time to time, and he'd rarely push back in a public setting. 'He was never unprofessional about it—not to my face anyway. Turns out, when I wasn't in the room, it was a different story.' She still couldn't untangle it all in her head—if people hadn't liked her because she was abrupt and lacked charm, or if Liam had been sabotaging her behind her back all that time, or some mixture of the two.

'God, Sasha, I'm sorry.'

'Why? You didn't do anything.'

'No, I suppose I'll call you out right to your face.'

'At least you're honest. Anyway, when I left, Liam walked right into my old job.'

'What, he got away with it?'

'I'd already decided I was coming home, no point in rescuing my reputation, no fight left in me—the relationship had been dead in the water a while.' She'd moved on already, even then, and certainly now. But the sting of betrayal was still there.

She brushed the thought aside—Liam was not welcome in this OR. Cam was holding her hand as if it was some prized jewel. Sasha didn't want to be anywhere else, with anyone else, doing anything else. She lifted Cam's hand to her mouth, pressed a kiss to the inside of his thumb, on the callus there. The graze of his strong, scarred hand against her sensitive lips—she felt that everywhere.

'It feels like we're close,' he said. 'The robot re-brand—not quite there yet, but getting closer.'

She turned his hand over, traced the lines with her fingers. 'Yeah. Getting there.'

'If the funding comes through, if other departments have their own Anne Hathaway…'

She laughed—this man, she'd only known him a month, but he'd changed everything. Just talking to him, barely even touching, and she felt so much… joy. That was what it was. He made her laugh, made her feel seen and understood, made her hope for so much more.

He was saying, 'It'll be important that other surgeons are up to speed with how to explain it to patients.'

He was right, and that was the tip of the iceberg. She let the thought bring her back down to earth. 'If we get the funding—' she stood up '—it's going to be really busy—training all the different teams, setting up the protocols. I'm still just finding my way around, getting to know who's who and how things are done here. Are the other surgeons going to jump on board with this comms strategy?'

It was the imposter syndrome talking, the fear that she was unlikeable, that this whole thing could fall down on her being not nice enough, not personable enough, too driven and strident and abrupt. She'd step on the wrong person's toes and, because she was still so new here, she'd probably have no idea what exactly she'd done wrong, but it'd all fall apart anyway. And then she'd forever wonder where she'd gone wrong, circling regrets and what-ifs, wishing for a do-over.

All Cam said was, ‘You’ll be amazing.’

She shot him a sceptical look.

‘Vivian Stirling knows what she’s doing,’ he said, more statement than question.

‘She does.’ There were other doctors involved now, lining up their patients to be a part of it, surgeons eager for a slice of the pie. People Sasha didn’t know as well—but so long as Vivian knew them.

‘And she trusts you, so…’

It was a flawless logic, but it didn’t magic away her unease. ‘So if I make a hash of it, that’s even worse.’

‘You’re not going to make a hash of anything.’ He pulled her closer, and when she resisted, he turned and pressed a kiss to the nearest bit of her—the swell of her right hip. ‘We should go get some dinner, think about other things. Maybe our subconscious minds will solve this riddle while we’re distracted.’

‘Distraction sounds good.’

‘Hm, doesn’t it?’ He was nuzzling her thigh now, doing all sorts of wicked things to her. Did he realise? Probably, given the flush of his cheeks, the satisfied glint in his eye. ‘Permission to distract the hell out of you.’

‘Yeah?’

His hands grew firm on her hips. ‘That scent is distracting the hell out of me. Only fair I reciprocate.’ He had the tie of her scrubs between his teeth, tugging them loose while she watched.

Just like that, she was pulsing with want, with the energy and anticipation of desire. He stroked his thumb along the bare skin of her belly, just above her waistband, sparking every nerve. She wriggled, letting her scrubs drop, and Cam gave a hungry moan, pressing kisses to her now bare thighs, his face cool against her heat. He hummed against her core and she swore. He chuckled, and the vibration of it made her buck forward.

'That's not very professional language, Dr McBride.'

'Quite right,' she said, voice quivering. 'My apologies.'

'Is the pressure of the job getting to you?' On the word pressure, he gave a little more.

'I do my best work under pressure,' she stuttered, gasping already.

'I have to see you.' He gave up the game and tugged down her underwear. 'God, the scent of you.' He lifted her leg, planting her foot on the arm of his chair. 'That's better.'

She felt brilliantly exposed, cool air kissing her most sensitive places, and then the firm plane of his tongue sent a sharp pulse through her. He traced the lines of her body, a steady pressure, warm and slick. He grazed his fingers up the inside of her thigh, anticipation building.

Then he paused, looked up at her, and slipped his fingers into his own mouth. His lips were shiny with her desire. He slid his fingers free and teased her with them. 'May I?'

'God, yes.' She arched as he pressed inside, and then his mouth was on her again. His steady stroke was almost too slow. Her body begged for more, rolling into his touch. She bit down hard to keep from crying out. The operating suites were all empty at this hour, and no one would be nearby, but the last thing she wanted was to call the attention of some cleaner or technician or whoever happened to be around. Not while her clothes were in a pool on the floor and Cam had his head between her thighs, playing her body like an instrument. She was right on the brink, teetering there with each brilliant stroke of his tongue, his fingers. The graze of his five-o'clock shadow on her thighs. The occasional, incidental nudge of his nose just above her core. And then he paused for breath, and it was that, the warm breeze of him panting against her, that pushed her over the edge. He must have felt the grip of her body; it was as if he knew exactly what she needed, and her whole body shook with it.

'That's the way,' he whispered, soothing her through the last shocks of pleasure until she wanted to do nothing but collapse limp against him.

'Anyone could walk in,' she said.

'Hmm,' he hummed into her core. 'Seems a shame to hide such beauty.'

Oversensitive all of a sudden, she wriggled away and snatched up her clothing and dressed in a rush. 'We should, um, go.'

'Good thing the robotic assistant doesn't have a recording function.'

'He does actually, but don't worry; it's not switched on.'

'Next thing you'll tell me it's got some kind of AI learning function.' He adjusted himself in his trousers.

'And you accidentally just taught it some new skills?'

He laughed. 'They do have gadgets for that, I believe.'

'Hah!'

'Now there's an out-of-the-box rebrand idea.'

'All the male surgeons will take it as an insult to their prowess.'

'Well, I for one am not opposed to a battery-powered team-mate.'

'Want to come back to mine?' she said, the question slipping out before she could think better of it. So much for taking it slow, safe and sensible.

Her new apartment was a mess. She'd moved in four days ago, and it was full of boxes still—hardly ready for visitors.

'I haven't finished unpacking,' she said, giving him a way out if he wanted it.

'I'd love to.'

'Okay.' Was that relief she felt? Something warm and bright seemed to lift her up and fill her chest to bursting.

He grinned. 'Okay.'

Cam had been meaning to swing by HR for that conversation for days, but work kept getting in the way. Work, and snatching up every moment with Sasha before and after and occasionally even during the day. They were playing it cool on the ward, acting like indifferent colleagues over at Outpatients, but all that pretending only stoked the fires, and the moment her office door was closed he had to have her.

They were being careful. Well…ever since the operating theatre they'd been *more* careful. Locked doors, at a bare minimum. But this couldn't go on forever.

He was running a few minutes ahead and if he could shave a bit of time off his next patient, that, on top of the break coming up—he resolved to go to HR, not concoct an excuse to lock himself in a room with Sasha. Again.

Then he saw his patient's name. Gareth Clarke. Shit. Cam had made sure another physio took care of Mr Clarke, but with seasonal illness everyone had needed to shift things around today, and Cam had said a blanket yes to the scheduling changes, completely forgetting he had reason to avoid this one patient.

But there was no avoiding Gareth Clarke today. Cam read over his notes—two weeks of in-patient care and the wound was healing well. The oedema would be central to their session today—that and managing expectations. But first, Cam found a quiet corner to stash his wheelchair.

A couple of quick stretches didn't take the edge

off Cam's discomfort, but he managed to walk in with minimal limping. 'How are you, Mr Clarke?'

'Gareth,' the man corrected.

'Gareth, I know you've been working with Ben, but he's away today.'

'I've been doing his exercises—the wife does them with me every visit. She says losing my arm is helping her avoid osteoporosis, so that's something. Wait on, have we met before?'

Cam nodded, masking the low-level panic rising at the memory. 'There was a mistake—I misread some paperwork. Sorry about that.'

'It was right after, eh?'

'Yeah, I was under the impression you'd requested a service—'

'A disability thing?' Mr Clarke was the first one to say the d-word, so that was definite progress. 'I was going to ask Ben about it, but I didn't know the name of it.'

'Disability Advocacy Services.'

'What does that mean exactly?' Mr Clarke sat, cradling his elbow just above the compression bandage.

'We support folks navigating the medical system, making and attending appointments, helping with medical jargon, ensuring patients are informed and their wishes are heard.'

'That sounds good.'

'Well, if there's anything top of mind right now…?'

'Just keen to be a bit less useless, you know? The

wife's working full-time, with me out, so she's up to her eyes, and when I get home, I don't want to be a burden.'

'You're not a burden.'

'I do the exercises, but my balance is a bit off. Will that be better once I get my prosthetic?'

'You're clearly motivated and that's a big part of recovery—that acceptance and drive to move forward, rather than go back to how things were.'

Mr Clarke was nodding, then stopped. 'Didn't you have a wheelchair?'

'I do use one most of the time.'

'You just don't see a lot of it around—people working, people with disabilities. Well, you know, stuff like wheelchairs and this.' He waved his stump. 'I'm thinking of getting a hook just to make it even more in people's faces.'

Interesting. Most of Cam's patients, and not just the amputees, were keen to get 'back to normal', to function, or at least to appear to, as if they'd never had a major surgery. People wanted to seem 'normal', even if doing so cost them dearly.

But this guy was willing to stand out. 'I kind of like the idea,' he was saying, 'always did, even before, you know?'

'What idea?' Cam asked.

'I'm a wharfie, but I can recite Seamus Heaney, Langston Hughes, a bit of Shakespeare. When people underestimate you and you blow their expectations out of the water—I love that.'

Mr Clarke was clearly adjusting to his new reality—his humour and honesty were all good signs. Cam had been so worried that seeing a wheelchair had set Mr Clarke back that day. But perhaps, in a weird way, it had helped, seeing someone working, professional, independent, and disabled.

They were running short on time, but after massaging the oedema Cam gave him some progressions—the amputation meant unequal weight distribution, so strength and balance were more important than ever. The last thing the man needed was further injury

'The missus is going to love one-legged squats and what are the lunges called again?'

'Bulgarian split squats.'

'I'd better write that down.'

'I'll print them out for you.'

'Good man.'

CHAPTER TWELVE

SASHA WAS UPDATING her notes, borrowing one of the computers at the nurses' station between post-operative appointments, and hoping to cross paths with Cam. She was spending more time on the ward than was strictly necessary, but they wouldn't have to keep it secret much longer, and then everything would be easier.

'We got it.' Vivian sidled up to her and spoke low. 'Don't tell anyone, we're just waiting on the official confirmation, but I know a guy.'

Sasha found herself being spontaneously side-hugged. 'The funding?'

Vivian held her finger to her lips in the universal sign for shush. But she was grinning. 'I knew bringing you here was the right choice. We'll announce officially—I'm hoping later today. The higher-ups want to make it a whole thing. Cake and speeches.'

'Sounds like a wedding.'

'Doesn't get more romantic than funding public healthcare, if you ask me.' Vivian overacted a sappy sigh, but her smile was genuine. 'I've copied you in to the final application, the updated list with everyone's patients and contributions. Let me know which surgeons I still need to introduce you to.'

Sasha opened it up in another window. Vivian had walked away before she needed clarification on anything, and it wasn't difficult for Sasha to search up the patients' files. For the unfamiliar surgeons, staff photos supplied faces to match the names, and they were all vaguely familiar.

The overall effect was a strong sense of *woah, that's a lot*. Which was, of course, intended. This hospital was going to make damn good use of these machines. So many people would benefit. No one could argue with the long-term and wide-spread impact of shorter hospital stays, lower risk of infection and fewer complications. Some of the patients' names were familiar. Some surprising. Mr Clarke had been released only a couple of days ago. Dr Pierce had picked him up a week ago—Vivian had encouraged Sasha to offload some patients, to balance her increasing responsibilities, and Sasha had been more than willing to hand over the man's care to another surgeon, after her mistake that day. She didn't know Dr Pierce very well but saw in the notes that he'd done a phone consult this morning, and the consent had come through within an hour.

Every i was dotted, every t crossed. Still, Vivian had copied Sasha in for a reason. They both cared about doing this right. So Sasha would read through it all, not only to flag any queries or concerns, but to familiarise herself with this thing she'd put her name to.

* * *

Cam was on his way to HR when a familiar nurse stopped him in the hallway. 'There's pizza in the break room.'

'Nice. Enjoy.' He wasn't so easily dissuaded from his mission. He'd said he would have this conversation—he *wanted* to have this conversation, to make sure this thing with Sasha was all above board and didn't throw a spanner in their work lives. It was her career most likely harmed by the association, of which he was painfully aware. Surgeons had status with a capital S. Physios, not so much. Disabled physios who did advocacy work on the side, which often meant rubbing powerful people up the wrong way… Well, Cam did it with a smile and got away with plenty, rarely made anything like an enemy. He knew he was liked, respected too, but he wasn't a surgeon. When people found out about their relationship, Sasha's colleagues would be more surprised than impressed.

He *wanted* to have this conversation, yes. But it wasn't as simple as that. Nina's surgery had been pulled up—she'd messaged him this morning. She was in the mix with this funding application, which might be a good thing, or might be a red flag. Cam honestly didn't know which.

He thought of Mr Clarke, of how it had all turned out for the best. And Mr Tait, how he'd come around to TMR in time—not because Sasha had talked him into it. But there was no denying how compelling Sasha could be. She might not even realise she'd pushed someone into something. She had good intentions, no question about that, but good intentions weren't always enough. He'd seen that arrogant streak, the one that made her believe she knew what was best for her patients, knew *better than* her patients. Perhaps that particular streak was inevitable in a good surgeon.

But in a partner, it gave Cam pause. He'd been with well-intentioned women before. He'd helped them see their flawed assumptions, coaxed them to question, shifted mindsets—or he'd thought he had. They'd only said what he'd wanted to hear, kept up the façade for as long as they could. Or, in Twyla's case—another physio, who really should have known better—refused to accept his limits, accused him of not even trying: *it's not even a three-hour walk; people take their toddlers.*

But that had been at the end. At the start, she'd said all the right things. They all had. Was Sasha going to do the same? In the first rush of lust and connection, listen closely, impress him with her willingness to understand, falling over herself to do better? And then the moment she had something to lose—or gain, in this case: her funding application—would she conveniently forget about informed consent and agency and autonomy?

He had to live it, every day, fight to be seen as fully human, a competent adult. She was able-bodied and could simply forget—choose to forget. No one ever doubted her ability to understand her own medical decisions. No one dared push her into something she didn't fully want.

But he was still going to see HR. Because he'd fallen in love with Sasha. Because he'd told her he would have this conversation. Because *she* had a lot to lose here, and she was willing to take that risk on him, and if he had to look past the perhaps inevitable lapses of any able-bodied person, then he'd do that, because what was the real alternative here? It'd hurt like hell, every time, but she'd never do it on purpose and that had to count for something.

The nurse was still standing in his path in the hallway. 'They want us all there,' she said. 'Some big announcement.'

'Now?'

'Yeah. Apparently there's cake, too. This better not be further staffing cuts.'

Cam started to turn his chair. 'Might just be about parking again.'

'They wouldn't bring the execs in for parking.'

Curiosity won out, and he joined the growing crowd in the break room. Sasha was there already. He was immediately aware of her, knew exactly where she was standing in relation to him, exactly what she was doing. The way she drew his attention made him marvel at no one's noticing anything between them. And marvel, too, that no one else seemed to see her light, see how smart and beautiful and brilliant she was. All his doubts and fears vanished the moment he was near her. She wasn't like any woman he'd dated before. Sasha McBride was incapable of faking anything.

Sasha was aware of Cam as soon as he entered the room. She was plotting a path to him. People were eating pizza and speculating about the news. The execs hadn't arrived yet, so maybe she had time to get to him. Explain. But what was there to explain? A whole lot of her colleagues had banded together to get this application over the line, had got their patients' consent; it was all there in the paperwork. To anyone else, the only red flags were the dates—this had all been done alarmingly quickly. A month ago, that was all Sasha would have noticed. But a lot had happened in that time.

Cam had happened. He'd made her see things she never used to notice, made her hesitate—not doubt herself, but *check* herself. But it was a whole step further to start *checking* others.

Cam was parked right by the door, unable to get further into the room, and as Sasha arrived at his side, more people arrived. She held the door open for them and caught Cam's eye, nodding out to the hallway.

The door shut behind them and a strange silence fell. Suddenly she was nervous. Instead of what she was planning to say, she asked, 'How'd it go with HR?'

'Oh, I haven't got there yet. I was hoping to swing by today, but then this—what is this?'

She felt as if she'd tripped, the ground that had seemed so safe and solid beneath her feet suddenly not where she'd thought it was. Cam hadn't talked to HR? He'd seemed so willing, or was she misremembering that whole conversation? Had she pushed him into it? Had she just seen what she wanted to see? Told herself what she wanted to hear—that they were the real deal, that he wanted this just as badly as she did? She'd rushed into the whole relationship without meaning to, her stupid, needy heart desperate for connection, and he'd been right there with her. Or so she'd thought.

But he hadn't talked to HR. It had been days. He'd put it off. He'd suggested it, but he must have had second thoughts—he didn't really want to do this. And fair enough, maybe no one ever really wanted to talk to HR, but Sasha couldn't tamper down that old voice in her head. She was too much. She wanted too much. She expected too much. Too outspoken, too confident, too fast.

'What's going on?' Cam asked again. Then Vivian appeared down the hall, execs in tow, and he guessed: 'Oh, the funding.'

Sasha met his gaze, hoping he wouldn't see all her hurt and fear in the time it took to nod. Speaking her answer wasn't an option. She pivoted to hold the door open—and to hide her face from Cam's suddenly concerned expression. He could switch on the kindness, the caring, and if he did, she'd be putty in his hands. How many times had she seen him do that with patients? And she'd fallen for it, thought it meant more than it did. He was a nice guy. But he was nice to everyone. Sasha wasn't *that* special.

CHAPTER THIRTEEN

WHILE VIVIAN MADE the announcement, Cam was aware of two things: all these people crammed together in this room were raising the temperature and CO2 at an alarming rate, and Sasha, right beside him, had her arms crossed, her body turned ever so subtly away—something wasn't right.

Vivian Stirling was doling out the thank-yous, praising Sasha to the skies, but beside him, she remained tense. Maybe she just didn't like the spotlight. She waved away the option of making a speech, saying only, 'It was a team effort.'

Then one of the execs took over, explaining what it would mean—changes to surgical teams, the training modules and transition process. It was all pitched as opportunities, but it was blatantly obvious, to Cam at least, that the higher-ups weren't here for a slice of celebration. Getting this funding would mean some real changes, and people hated change, and this was less a party and more placation, more pleading: *don't panic!*

When the speeches were done, the cake was cut, and Cam slipped away. He had no appetite for cake or anything else on offer in that room. These changes weren't going to impact his job much. No other reason to hang about. No questions about the technology or training or rosters. And any questions he might have asked, he wouldn't get a straight answer on those today.

Sasha answered about a thousand questions before she managed to ask the one she needed to: 'What happens if one of these patients rescinds their consent?'

Vivian's head snapped up. 'Who?'

'It's more a hypothetical question than…' They weren't *alone* alone in the slowly emptying break room, but no one was listening, right there beside them. 'Mr Clarke comes to mind. Pierce signed him off this morning.'

'Best talk to Pierce, then.' Someone else was coming over; Sasha couldn't blame Vivian for a less-than-crystal-clear answer.

Plus, Pierce was still there, squeezing out a teabag with his fingers. He gave a slight hiss. 'Pass the milk?' he said, seeing Sasha approach.

She got it out of the fridge. 'I was surprised to see Mr Clarke on the list.'

'It's the best thing for him; he'll thank us in the long run.'

'He only just went home, and now he's up for another surgery?'

'Which one's Clarke?' He downed half his tea in one gulp.

'Port worker, upper-limb amputee.'

'Are you questioning whether I know how to consent a patient, Dr McBride?'

'No, only you signed off quite a few in a very short period of time.'

'Are you serious? I'm the one who got this application over the line, and you're getting all the glory, and now I'm…' He tossed the remains of his tea down the drain and marched off. 'So much for being thanked.'

Shit. Sasha had handled that badly. Pierce was someone she needed to work with. Had she really been rude or had he overreacted? Then there was that niggling question in the back of her mind: would he have reacted that way if she were a man? But she brushed it away—there was little point in wondering because what could she do about it?

Well, there was one thing she could do: talk to Mr Clarke. She could swing by his next physio appointment. But that was days away and might be cancelled with his treatment changing so dramatically.

Cam popped into her head, as he often did. He'd probably gone home by now—she should do the same. He hadn't talked to HR. He'd told her what she wanted to hear. He'd been caught up in the moment—she didn't even blame him. She was too much, too needy, too honest. And maybe he wasn't honest enough. If he'd been there, chatting with the nurses, waiting for her, she might have pushed all that from her mind and gone home with him. Let him distract her. Pretend she wasn't terrified.

But what was the point in pretending? Delaying the hurt, the disappointment for later? And she was no good at pretending; it'd seep in, slowly poison every touch, every kind word, with cruel doubts, echoes of the past, all those truths Cam was too nice to say.

She put on her coat and headed out into the night.

She walked down the ramp, even though it was the long way—or because it was the long way. She was in no hurry to get home to her empty apartment, where she'd spent so little time, but the memories she had there were almost entirely with Cam. He'd helped unpack a couple of boxes—things from her mum's, keepsakes from her childhood: old yearbooks, a school-uniform shirt covered in signatures, certificates and glowing report cards.

She rounded the corner where all the smokers went—just beyond the hospital boundary. She heard Cam's voice before she spotted him: 'I can make it work, even if I have to shift things around.'

'I don't want to put you out,' a woman in a wheelchair beside him said.

'Hi.' Sasha let her presence be known.

'Oh.' Cam cleared his throat. 'Sasha. I mean Dr McBride. This is Nina. She's on your list.'

'Nina... Sheffield?' Sasha's tired brain supplied the name like one last trick. She couldn't remember anything else about the woman. 'Who's your surgeon?'

'Pierce,' Nina said. 'First thing tomorrow. I'm a

bit nervous. I don't usually smoke any more, but what the heck?'

Sasha just nodded.

'Nina and I went to school together,' Cam said.

'Oh, right.' Sasha shouldn't be surprised—this city was infamous for everyone knowing everyone. Two degrees of separation, people said. Sasha had been overseas since halfway through medical school—long enough that it didn't apply to her.

'We were both told we'd never walk,' Nina said. 'So we did it anyway.' She gave a laugh, but it wasn't very convincing. 'Well, for a while I did. I better get some sleep. Thanks for the company, Cam.'

'I'll pop by in the morning,' Cam said.

Nina nodded but didn't say another word, heading up the ramp and out of sight.

He started moving—in the direction of Sasha's apartment, not the bus station, so presumably he would come home with her if she wanted him to. And she did. Of course she did. She was freaking out about him not talking to HR, reading into it, maybe making a mountain out of a molehill. Probably. This was all so new, all so fast. It was natural to be scared, to waver.

'Nina has spina bifida,' Cam said. 'Hasn't walked in years. She doesn't have much sensation in her legs. I'm no expert, but phantom pain is unlikely to be a major issue after her amputation, and yet she's lined up for TMR, and suddenly her surgery has been brought up the list. Tell me the truth: they're training a new team, might as well do it on someone who won't realise if they mess it up.'

'What?'

'Tell me the truth: do these patients know what they're signing up for? Is it for them or for the funding? The shiny new technology and the glory?'

'You really think I'm in this for the glory, Cam? I don't know Nina's case, but robotic-assisted surgery is safer, more accurate, lower risk…you know all that. There's so much to gain here.'

He fixed her with a look that demanded more.

'What do you expect me to do? I'm already checking every case; it's a fine line, going over my colleagues' heads. I've already alienated Pierce, questioning Mr Clarke's consent.'

'Gareth Clarke?'

'Yeah.'

'But he just went home. He's picked out a hook hand. He's planning pranks. He doesn't want another surgery—he doesn't *need* another surgery.'

'Apparently he's changed his mind.'

'Apparently? It's your name on the application, Sasha.'

'And Stirling. And Norris.'

'Right,' he said, and fell silent. The low hum of his wheels spinning was the only sound between them.

She was almost jogging to keep up with him. Was he going too fast for her on purpose or was he just so furious he didn't even realise, all that anger like fuel propelling him along the path? 'I'll look into Nina's case tonight,' Sasha said.

'And the rest?'

'I have to be careful—I can't undermine everyone I work with, checking and re-consenting all the patients on the application. I have to trust my colleagues or…' She gestured at the hospital they'd barely left behind them. 'Or none of this works.'

'This *works* for a select few.'

It felt like a body blow. She worked incredibly hard, sacrificed almost every other facet of her life for this work, and he was saying it wasn't good enough. 'Robotic assistants will make it work just a little bit better for a few more people.'

'Sasha, you need to hit pause on this.' His tone was pleading now. As if he didn't want to hurt her—though that didn't make it any less painful.

'The robotic assistant isn't the problem. Dr Pierce's team know what they're doing. And surely she's better off getting her amputation sooner rather than later.'

'Surgeon knows best? Always the smartest person in the room; it's easy to forget the others are still people, people who should get to decide for themselves, even if they don't have fancy letters after their name.'

It had never occurred to her before, not until that moment, but could Cam be bothered by her being a doctor? That the thought hadn't once crossed her mind, till now, in itself was remarkable—it had definitely been an issue in the past. Outranking and out-earning a guy had never once improved the dating experience. But with Cam, it hadn't ever seemed like a factor. Until now. Her voice failed her.

He stopped his chair so suddenly—that had to hurt his hands.

She asked, without thinking, 'Are you all right?'

He only shook his head. 'We could have…' His voice was thick and cracking. 'We could have been…us.'

Those words, she knew even as he said them, would haunt her.

CHAPTER FOURTEEN

CAM'S HANDS WERE BURNING. He'd been stupid, and he'd likely pay for it for days.

And he didn't just mean the raw skin on the inside of his thumbs; he'd trusted Sasha. He'd thought she was different. The way they'd clicked, how working together felt so easy and natural and just *right*.

He was around a corner, safely out of Sasha's sight line—not that he expected her to look back at him. Getting himself all the way to the bus and then home at the other end, it was too much to ask right now. Too far. He let his chair roll to a stop and considered his options. A taxi, maybe. He checked the time—only slightly after the rostered shift change in ED. Maybe Neroli was finishing work. He texted her and, adjusting his grip, made a slow and awkward journey back to the hospital.

As he retraced the path he and Sasha had just taken, every word seemed to leap up off the pavement as if they'd left a physical trail. Sasha's excuses and explanations, his anger and disappointment and…betrayal. That was what it felt like. He'd trusted her. She'd betrayed—not just him, but herself, her integrity, her own values. The very day they'd met she'd spoken of honesty. From the start, they'd agreed on that, *shared* that. He'd thought it might be enough. He'd hoped…

The emergency department was frantic. He wheeled around the full waiting room and found a spot, out of the way. He was about to give up and call a taxi when his sister appeared. She skirted around half a dozen sick, sad, sore and tired people to get to him. 'Are you okay?'

'Yeah, no, I'm…' His voice was giving him away. He was not okay. He didn't have a third-degree burn or a broken bone; he wasn't having a heart attack or a stroke. He was fine. But he was not okay.

'I'm meant to be finished, but…' Neroli looked around at the chaos. 'Do you want a ride home?'

'Yeah, but I can wait. Nowhere to be.' And no one waiting for him.

'Okay, I'll try not to be long. You sure you're all right?'

'Of course,' he said, pivoting away as if he were getting in someone's way; there was little point lying to his sister, but now wasn't the moment to tell her the truth.

What, exactly, he would tell her, or should tell her, that was something to ponder while he watched the sea of humanity churn for however long it took his sister to tie up the loose threads at the end of her shift. He couldn't help but compare his own steady stream of patients with the immediacy of this environment. There was a whole different flavour of…

fear. An imminent threat to life and limb, whereas Cam was used to the looming menace of chronic pain and disability.

Neroli came and got him only half an hour later; long enough that Cam wasn't feeling so sorry for himself any more. Long enough that he'd forgotten about his hands and, habit of a lifetime, started wheeling his chair same as ever.

Neroli clearly noticed his pain, the jerk of her head clear in his periphery, but he kept his eyes on the busy corridor between them and the elevator.

'Where are your gloves?' she asked.

'At home. It's not often I need them.'

'You gonna show me the damage or what?' She reached for his hand when they arrived at the elevators, and for a moment he thought she might believe there was nothing more going on for him than friction burns. Then she said, 'An orthopaedic surgeon would be overqualified for abrasions of this nature, but she does live conveniently close by.'

'I doubt she'd be pleased to see me right now.'

'What did you do?'

'Held her to her own standards.'

'What?'

'I know.' He punched the elevator button a second time. 'The audacity.'

'Cam.'

The elevator opened, revealing three other people, one of whom was vaguely familiar, so they travelled in silence. Not another word between them until they were alone in Neroli's car. Plenty of time for Cam to figure out what he wanted to say.

'There's this funding application, a collaboration between departments, but it's Sasha's name on it.'

'The robotic-assistant thing,' Neroli guessed, because of course she'd heard—the hospital wasn't that big. 'I thought that was a done deal.'

'Done as in cooked.'

'They're saying it'll be great long-term, once everyone's up to speed. Quicker recovery times, shorter stays. It's not just staff shortages causing that backlog.' She nodded in the general direction of the emergency department, driving them out of the parking building. 'I had four patients waiting for beds just now. Three of them are probably in ED overnight. When I start my shift tomorrow, I guarantee at least one of them is still there. You know what our wait times are like.'

'I'm all for the robot,' Cam said. 'That's not the issue.'

'Okay. So what's the issue?'

'Unnecessary and unwanted procedures for the sake of ticking boxes.'

'Sasha McBride is signing off on unnecessary and unwanted procedures?'

'No, it was another surgeon, but it was in service of her funding application, and she doesn't see the problem. Or if she sees it, she's not willing to do anything about it.'

'Right.'

'I really thought she got it—that the individual matters, that a person's bodily autonomy is not a spanner in the works, it *is* the works. This whole jam is in service of health, of people, of doing better. Not sacrificing a few vulnerable and, as it happens, disabled folks in service of the greater good.'

Neroli pulled out into the flow of traffic, and silence settled between them for a moment before she said, 'Well, shit.'

'Yep,' Cam agreed.

'You went and fell for a surgeon.'

'What?'

'I should probably take some of the blame,' Neroli said, as if talking to no one but herself. 'I was fooled by her...charm's not the word for it. Amputating that dock worker's arm in the field was pretty impressive.'

'That dock worker was healing well, and now he's signed up for a surgery he neither wants nor needs because cross-departmental procedures like targeted muscle reinnervation look good on funding applications.'

'Targeted muscle reinnervation?' Neroli sounded impressed—perhaps she was surprised Cam knew what those words even meant, or could be she was impressed by the procedure itself. 'I'm no expert,' she went on, 'but isn't he likely to have less pain, more agility, maybe even one of those fancy, mind-reading prosthetics that can turn on taps and button buttons.'

'Okay, but—'

'Washing and dressing—that's bodily autonomy in some pretty key ways.'

'Are you seriously explaining that to me right now?' Cam asked.

'Sorry.'

He sighed. 'No, I'm sorry. You're not the one who—'

'It's your first fight, isn't it?' Neroli said, as if it weren't a question at all. 'It feels like the end, like your heart's been yanked out of your chest and now your internal organs are all blowing in the wind for any passer-by to throw a casual punch at.'

'That is a graphic image.'

She shrugged, put her hand on his seat back, and twisted to check her blind spot before changing lanes. Dropping her hand to his shoulder, she gave it a squeeze. 'She's only been here a short while, and those funding applications, to get them over the line, it's always a matter of choosing your battles.'

'I don't think I can be with someone who doesn't choose this battle.'

'Bull shit.'

'What?'

'The wound is fresh. Don't make any lifelong decisions right away.'

'You think I'm going to change my mind?' He couldn't believe what he was hearing. From his sister. The one person in the world who knew him the best.

'I think you're blaming an individual for a systemic issue. I think you're blowing up the best relationship you've had, maybe ever, because it's scary. I think you're trying to protect yourself from everyone who's hurt you before—and fair enough. But protecting yourself can backfire.'

'From good intentions and no follow-through. Something everyone I ever dated had in common.'

'Well, I won't pretend I know Sasha as well as you do.' Neroli was turning into his street. 'And who am I to talk? In the last ten hours I forcibly restrained two patients, lied to a domestic abuser about his child's care, performed emergency surgery on several people who gave their consent while clearly in no fit state to make significant decisions, and said "you'll just feel a small pinch" so many times even I'm starting to believe the BS.'

'That's different,' Cam said.

'Not *that* different.' She pulled over outside his house—the house that used to be her house before she shacked up with her boyfriend three streets over.

Cam forced his tired body to get out of the car, into his chair, into the house. Had he even thanked Neroli for driving him home? He flicked her a quick text: Thanks for the lift.

She replied, Put some kawakawa on your hands.

Sasha had back-to-back surgeries in the morning; this was no time for a sleepless night.

We could have been us.

She rolled away from his voice.

Surgeon knows best?

His accusation, all sarcasm and disappointment, chased her across the pillow, and either she was imagining it or his scent lingered there from the nights he'd stayed over. But then she remembered asking him if he'd talked to HR.

Oh, I haven't got there yet.

How could she ever trust someone who could switch it on and off at will? How could she ever know he was for real? She was mourning this thing as if it were so much more than it was—more than it was for Cam, anyway.

We could have been us.

This was no good. She threw off the covers, tore off the Cam-scented pillowcase, and went to find a fresh one.

Some sleepy tea might be a good idea. There was just enough street light to safely navigate around the sofa and avoid bumping into Cam's bookshelves on her way to the kitchen counter. While the kettle rose to a boil, she stepped out onto the wee balcony. No moon tonight. The stars were bright, though. She spotted the Southern Cross and remembered learning how to find South—follow the long axis, imagine a line intersecting the two pointers, and where those two meet…there it was, a hard left from where she stood, due South.

In Chicago, light pollution blotted out most of the stars, but she'd taken Liam to the Palos Preserves on a date one time—a dark-sky region just out of the city. He'd been amazed by how many stars were visible. Sasha had only been surprised how different they were from here, from home. Even Orion's Belt was upside down. She'd expected to recognise at least a few constellations, but the Illinois sky had felt like landing on another planet.

And then Liam had downloaded some app on his phone and sat there listing off familiar-sounding names, pointing out planets and constellations. She'd only felt more lost, more disconnected and distant—from him, from home, from herself in a weird way. Her identity had always been all wrapped up in *knowing* things, and, yeah, that was probably ego talking, but it had shaken her. The evening hadn't gone as she'd hoped; she'd been disappointed in herself, in Liam, in even the stars—ridiculous, really.

Maybe that was why Cam's words had hurt her so much: not because he was someone she couldn't do without, but because he'd pointed out her blind spots. He'd shown her there was another way to look at the situation.

The kettle boiling called her back inside. Sitting on the sofa in the dark, she nursed her cup, waiting for the tea to do its magic.

Are you questioning whether I know how to consent a patient?

Now it was Dr Pierce's voice invading her space.

I'm the one who got this application over the line, and you're getting all the glory.

She took a too-big gulp of tea, scalding her throat.

So much for being thanked.

She would deal with Pierce. She'd stepped on toes and dealt with men's egos her whole career; she could mend that particular fence. But she might have to make it worse first—she'd looked into Nina's case earlier in the evening. Amputation wasn't especially common for people with spina bifida, but trans-tibial amputation was a good option for chronic ulcers in non-ambulatory persons. Nina had requested amputation for the first time, according to her notes, eighteen months ago. She wanted this. She'd waited and probably had to fight for this.

But Cam probably had a point about TMR being unnecessary. And the team were inexperienced with the robotic assistant. Cam knew how hospitals worked, how decisions got made, how complicated it could get. TMR would mean a longer surgery, more sedation, and the risks accompanying anaesthesiology. The upside? On the slim chance Nina experienced phantom pain, TMR would reduce that to almost nothing.

That was what Sasha was telling herself when she visited Nina in Pre-op the next morning. 'How did you sleep?'

Nina laughed. 'In hospital, never well.'

Sasha had barely slept herself, but it wasn't beeping machines and corridor noises keeping her awake. 'How are the nerves?'

'Managed to sneak in a smoke before they brought me over. I'm all right. Keen to get this over and done with, to be honest. Waiting is the worst.'

'Did Cam come by already?'

'Not yet, but he will. He'll keep me company, keep me distracted until they wheel me in.'

Sasha couldn't help thinking that he was excellent at that—excellent company, and when it came to distractions…just the thought and her physical reaction was visceral. And then the sadness hit her over again. *We could have been us.*

They could have been. If only Sasha had been better, braver, stronger. She should have stalled the application, bought them a few days to double-check every patient on that list fully understood the pros and cons of their procedures.

The pros were easy: all the advantages of robotic-assisted surgery, plus getting operations sooner. As Nina put it, 'waiting is the worst'.

But for the cons: the surgical teams were new to this technology, and the funding application meant prioritising collaborations across departments, complex surgeries. And Sasha desperately wanted to believe that Gareth Clarke's and Nina's were the only ones of questionable necessity.

Wanting to believe a thing never did make it true though. She'd wanted to believe in this thing with Cam. That was why this hurt so much, because she'd believed in it. Believed that he liked, maybe even loved her. The real Sasha, the whole mess of her: unfiltered, direct, unwilling to play nice, too honest, too sure of herself, too much, too much, too much.

Cam had barely slept for the back-and-forth of his sister's voice, and Sasha's, his own words coming back to haunt him, and Nina's too. Then he'd gone and slept through his alarm, so by the time he got to the hospital, in a taxi he really couldn't afford, Nina was only moments away from going into Theatre. And instead of offering her comfort and reassurance, he apologised for being late, and she spent her last conscious moments reassuring him. It was all backwards and wrong.

'I'll come see you in Recovery afterwards,' he promised. He'd have to rearrange his schedule to ensure that was possible. Out in the hallway, he adjusted his gloves—they took most of the sting away, but it had been so long since he'd worn them regularly and the seam at his wrist was irritating.

He looked up and there was Sasha, walking towards him, fresh blue scrubs a reminder of the work she was about to do. She would hold lives in her hands. If they spoke now, if she went into the OR less than entirely focused—because of anything he said to her now—the stakes were too high. 'Hi,' he said.

'Cam—' She looked around as if worried they'd be heard. Seen.

'What do you have now?' he asked.

'Shoulder replacement.'

He nodded.

'Full schedule today.' She wasn't being rude, just professional and distant. And if it was over between them, this was how it would need to be going forward.

'I probably won't see you, then,' he said.

'Probably not.'

His heart wanted to leap out of his chest and fling itself at her, but somehow he kept his vital organs in place and a smile on his face. And went on with his day: first, a dangerously strong coffee and a bacon buttie from the hospital cafeteria. If ever there was a time for comfort food and caffeine in large quantities, this was it. Playing his part, keeping it professional and friendly, was going to demand his full faculties today, and he'd better save it for his patients. He parked up by the window and looked down over the park, the trees in full autumn colour—rich reds and bright yellows, the ground covered in orange leaves. He watched runners, school students, parents pushing prams, cyclists commuting into work, nurses leaving after the night shift.

'Exciting news yesterday, wasn't it?' Vivian Stirling sidled up to him, her own coffee in hand.

'Oh, ah, yeah.'

'Sasha mentioned you were working on some language, some helpful analogies to ensure our patients understand the robotic assistant better, to make it less unnerving.'

'We have some ideas—a start…'

A start, that was all they'd ever be now. A false start. A brilliant start, and then nothing.

Cam forced himself to finish the sentence: 'Haven't got it nailed down quite yet.' *Yet? Yet* sounded like hope. And hope made his chest ache. It was hard to imagine them working on this thing now, joking about Anne Hathaway and R2-D2.

'You make a great team,' Dr Stirling said. 'Your affinity with patients, her technical and clinical expertise. I'd love to see more such partnerships.'

He and Sasha were a great team…until they weren't. Until her funding application, her pet project, was on the line. Her reputation with her colleagues, that was what this was really about—risking her social capital when it really mattered.

Dr Stirling said, 'She's doing an ankle reconstruction this afternoon, if you want to observe—it's a bit different from the knee replacement. Might spark a different thought.'

'I have appointments most of the afternoon.'

'Even if you only pop by. Holistic care only really happens if we get better at looping each other in. Tricky to fit into these schedules—speaking of, I'd better go see my 9:00 a.m.'

Cam had already moved a couple of appointments to go see Nina. He might be able to make it happen. But did he want to? To see Sasha in action? Yes. To see her at all, in fact… He couldn't lie to himself, not on the little amount of sleep he'd had last night—of course he wanted to see her. He always wanted to see her.

Neroli had said this was their 'first fight', but Cam couldn't see a way through. His sister knew him better than anyone. Her words from last night came back to him: all those situations in ED where true informed consent was impossible.

Outside, a party bus went by—either starting very early or finishing very late. Its bright colours and glittery paint job made him think of *The Magic School Bus*. 'All aboard!'

But instead of miraculously being transported into the inner workings of some fascinating biological function, he finished his coffee and went to see his first patient.

CHAPTER FIFTEEN

POOR NIGHT'S SLEEP ASIDE, Sasha could not have planned today better if she'd tried. Back-to-back procedures and barely time to think about anything else.

Her final surgery was a little more high pressure than was perhaps ideal, with an audience of surgeons who'd recently finished their training simulations and, at most, had run a couple of real operations with the robotic assistant.

She'd seen Pierce on the way in, and attempted to heal the breach. In some ways, the sting of Cam's rejection was throwing everything else into perspective. Pierce would get over it in time. Rationally, it was a blip on the radar, it would pass, but knowing he was behind the glass, ready to find fault with the woman who'd found fault with him… Her heckles were just a tad raised. Inevitable.

Still, surgery took all her attention, and she soon forgot Pierce. She even forgot Cam, for a bit there. So it was something of a shock to come out and hear his voice.

* * *

Cam held his tongue for as long as he could bear it, listening to the surgeons' commentary. He could hear Sasha, too, through the speaker, her directions to her team clear and calm. But it was a one-way microphone, thank goodness.

'She won't be the darling forever,' one of them said.

'Do you think she doesn't like getting her hands dirty?' That was one of the plastic surgeons.

'I don't care how revolutionary this robo-tech is, I'm not giving up a good old-fashioned cut and thrust.'

'I was about to say, getting my hands dirty is half the fun. If I wanted to steer some high-tech machine, I'd have flown a fighter jet.'

'Didn't you used to have your pilot's licence?'

'You took us down to Queenstown one time—those were the days.'

'It was very generous.'

'It's important to show a bit of appreciation for the good folk you work with.'

'A bit of appreciation would go a long way.' That was Dr Pierce, the only orthopod in the room.

'How many operations did you line up for this funding application?'

'Doesn't matter—you're a white guy. Can't put your name first on anything these days.'

'I'm all for women getting fair recognition, pay, promotions, whatever, but operative word *fair*.'

'I got nothing against her, but she's been here,

what? Not even six weeks,' Pierce said. 'She doesn't know who's who or what's what. And a collaboration, it goes both ways. You can't be undermining other surgeons and then asking them for favours.'

'Feels a lot like ticking a quota.'

Cam felt slightly sick. Guilty, too. As if he should have spoken up long ago. As if it was too late now. As if he'd got it wrong yesterday, blaming Sasha for folding on her principles without realising what she had to deal with—*who* she had to deal with.

He had to talk to Sasha. But she was busy.

These guys, these surgeons, would they even listen to a lowly physio? The old hospital hierarchy benefited the lot of them, so they probably bought into all that—as if Cam needed further proof after the conversation he'd just been listening in on. Not eavesdropping, to be fair; he was right there, in plain sight, observing the surgery alongside them.

'The problem with women in charge is they're always trying to prove they deserve to be there, and if they really did deserve it, they wouldn't need to prove it over and over again.'

Cam found his voice: 'Or maybe it's because people accuse them of ticking a quota.'

'I didn't mean *all* women,' the guy who'd said the quota thing jumped to defend himself.

'She was blatantly trying to put her name beside my patients,' Pierce said, 'questioning consents as if she's the only one who can explain—as if she's so good at communicating.' He gave a bitter almost-laugh.

So he was the one who'd talked Mr Clarke into TMR and brought up Nina's operation. Never mind that Nina was awake in Recovery and glad to have it over and done with. 'Dr McBride isn't trying to steal your glory,' Cam said before he could second-guess himself. 'She couldn't be less interested in glory, and her name's already all over this application. If anything, she looks better with more collaborators. And she's been working with these robotic assistants for years; she didn't get where she is on privilege.'

Cam was so aware these were his colleagues—he had to work with some of these men and he was burning bridges, something he'd always avoided, but apparently he couldn't stop talking. 'She works incredibly hard, and isn't afraid of stepping on toes to make sure things are done right—what's best for the patient, that's it, all that matters to her. That's why she's running this—because she deserves it.'

'Hey, I didn't say she didn't deserve it.' One of the neurologists spoke up.

Silence rang like a bell.

Cam realised then that the surgery was over, or at least Sasha wasn't in the OR any more. Someone else was closing.

And the old boys' club of surgeons, who Cam had just insulted, even though they totally deserved it, were looking right past him. In itself, that wasn't unusual, but this wasn't standard-issue wheelchair invisibility.

Sasha was right behind him.

The neurologist came forward and started asking her a question about the procedure, and then everyone acted as if none of that had happened. Cam got out of there, left her to her fake fan club. These were the people questioning *her* integrity?

He still wanted to talk to her, but he needed to calm down first. How long had Sasha been standing there? Not that he'd said anything he didn't stand by, but she might not like him speaking on her behalf. Had he made things worse for her? She'd told him a little of how things had gone down with her ex back in Chicago, how he'd belittled her behind her back. What exactly had she heard just now?

He had to make it right. Had to show her he wasn't one of those guys. He wanted to be on her team—wanted her to never doubt it, never have to wonder if he was bad-mouthing her or sitting by while others picked her to pieces.

Somehow, he had to fix this.

Sasha didn't want to play nice. She wanted to go find Cam. But as Cam had so deftly put it, she'd stepped on some toes—with good intentions, yes, and it was a relief to hear Cam say it. But it hurt, too. Here was further proof he was a good guy. Here he was, standing up for her, standing up for what he believed, even though it wouldn't make him popular. His honesty—how could she doubt it?

He could be charming, friendly, positive, could turn it on even when he didn't feel like it—that was how.

But Cam's tirade, and, yes, that was the right word for what she'd just overheard, proved he wouldn't play nice if his integrity was on the line.

Which was exactly what had happened last night, when they'd fought—when they'd broken up. That was what it was, a break-up. But it had started out with Cam speaking up, being honest with her. And wasn't that exactly what she wanted, someone she could trust to say the hard thing when it needed to be said? Someone who would tell her the truth, even if it was easier not to?

She prided herself on being that person—even if it meant stepping on toes. Cam saw that in her, but he'd shown her the flip side of the coin: that playing nice wasn't necessarily dishonest; sometimes withholding a little was kinder, and sometimes pretending was just savvy.

And right now, talking to these surgeons as if she weren't livid, answering these questions, soothing their trod-on toes, was definitely savvy.

Thankfully, it was also brief, because she got called down to ED for a consult: a seventy-two-year-old woman, dislocation one-month post-operative from a hip replacement. Dr Lowe had already done a closed hip reduction, and was just waiting for a portable X-ray to confirm its success.

Mrs Johansen was still sedated, but her husband was doing a great job answering questions and asking them too. Did she truly need to stay overnight? Couldn't they come back for an outpatient appointment in the morning instead? Yes, she'd been doing all her exercises, following all the rules—it had been a momentary lapse, a thoughtless moment. The television remote had fallen on the floor and she'd bent down to pick it up. Next thing he'd known, she'd face-planted on the floor, gasping in pain, unable to move, barely able to speak. He'd called the ambulance, and lain down beside her, held her hand.

She'd had years of pain before her hip operations. A big believer in natural medicine, Mrs Johansen had delayed surgery as long as she could bear it. He'd talked her into it in the end, but these past few weeks, she'd been like her old self again. She'd started going back to the pottery studio, they'd seen plays and musicals, things she hadn't been able to sit through for the hip pain—things she'd loved and missed out on for years.

He carried her medicines and they made their way out to the elevators, Sasha assuring him that she would discharge his wife as soon as possible.

'Can I stay with her, if she has to be here overnight?' he asked.

'We'll see what we can do,' Sasha said. 'But she's going to need you in the coming days. An uninterrupted night's sleep in your own bed, come back fresh in the morning…?'

'Uninterrupted night's sleep? At my age?' He gave a laugh. 'Plus, it's nice to be needed.'

Sasha nodded, no argument there.

Mrs Johansen woke up in the elevator. 'The pain's gone. Are we going to the car, Ron?'

'Just waiting on Radiology,' Sasha said. 'Then we'll know what we're dealing with.'

'Who's she?'

Ron answered, 'She's the orthopaedic surgeon.'

'I'm not having another surgery, I'll tell you that much for free,' Mrs Johansen replied.

'I'm hopeful that won't be necessary.'

'I don't care you think it is "necessary".'

'It's probably soft tissue damage. A few sessions with the physio and you'll be good to go.'

'I'd rather go see my osteopath.'

On the orthopaedic ward, Sasha got the Johansens settled in a room. 'I'll be right back with some warm blankets.' As she walked away, she heard Ron say to his wife, 'Let me look after you, would you?'

Sasha felt that deep under her ribs. *That* was what she wanted. Not the traumatic dislocation of an endoprosthesis, but someone looking out for her, someone who knew her that well, knew what she wanted and feared, knew her quirks and preferences, and would stand by her through it all. And it went both ways—Sasha wanted to be that person for someone else. *It's nice to be needed,* Ron had said.

But Cam didn't need Sasha. He prized his independence, valued it perhaps more highly than most because he'd had to fight so hard for it. Still, she had started to hope he might…rely on her, at the very least. Let her be that person for him.

She opened the blanket warmer and pulled out two, then, hugging them to her chest, she carried them back, absorbing a little of the comfort. She felt raw, exposed and sore, sad, and tired too. Fatigue made everything worse. But if things were really over with Cam, a good night's sleep wasn't going to fix much. *We could have been us.* They weren't especially ambiguous words. *Could have been* implied an *if*—a condition she had not met. She did not qualify for the kind of dedication and loyalty, the *love* she was witnessing between Ron and his wife.

Back at the room, Mrs Johansen was trying to stand up. 'Let's just wait on the X-rays, then try walking.' Sasha tossed the blankets on the bed and reached, ready to catch her if she fell…but, holding Ron's hand, Mrs Johansen miraculously took a tentative step.

'If I can walk, I can leave. That was the deal last time,' she said.

'Well, yes, but that's with a physio assessing your movement and strength, and they've all gone home already.'

The woman shook off her husband's hand and took a few steps unassisted. But he was there, nearby, ready to help when he was needed.

It was an image of everything Sasha wanted—everything she couldn't have. This was love—the patience, the paying attention, the distance too, total trust and total readiness to jump in when needed.

'Can we sign out against medical advice?' Ron asked.

'The X-rays won't be long,' Sasha said, but Mrs

Johansen was up and walking—clearly the hip joint was in position. 'I'll come back with the paperwork and the imaging, and then we'll get you out of here.'

CHAPTER SIXTEEN

Sometimes, an idea arrived out of the blue, usually in the shower. One minute you were noticing the shampoo bottle was running low, the next, brainwave!

Then other times, an idea arrived in disconnected fragments, teasing, flirting, making you lean in and follow it, get your hopes up that it would come to anything at all.

Cam had a lot of tabs open: listicles and image searches of famous robots and sidekicks, manuals and medical journals for robotic assistants. No wonder doctors struggled to put this stuff in layman's terms—then again, would anyone take them seriously if they gave it *The Magic School Bus* treatment—helpful visual analogies, a dash of humour, and allowing for their audience not to have an advanced degree in the subject?

Cam was no Ms Frizzle, that was for sure. But this felt like the edge of an idea—maybe something worth pursuing.

He wanted to talk to Sasha, so he'd hung around after his shift. He didn't know what he might say, how he might begin, but their shared project seemed like safe territory.

Nina had had been moved to the orthopaedics ward, so Cam was keeping her company. She was sleeping, thankfully, or even in her heavily medicated state she'd have noticed something was up. Cam glanced down the hall every few moments, hoping to catch a glimpse of Sasha. Rehearsing what he might say and rehashing last night's conversation would make him spiral completely. But reading medical journals and chasing an idea that might turn out to be a helpful analogy was like brain GPS. It gave him a direction for his thoughts, a map and a route, something to pull him back on the road when an errant memory threatened to send him careening off a cliff.

Then there it was, all of a sudden, the destination. All the bits of ideas, the maybe-somethings, coalesced into one. This was it.

He had to find Sasha.

'I'll come by tomorrow,' he murmured to his sleeping friend, then rolled out into the hallway. No sign of Sasha…or anyone. Which, at this hour, wasn't entirely surprising. He'd lost track of time. Had Sasha already given up and gone home? Given up on what exactly? Did he really think she was waiting for him?

And then he saw her, hugging blankets from the warmer, disappearing into one of the single rooms. Cam inched closer.

‘If I can walk, I can leave. That was the deal last time,’ someone was saying.

‘Well, yes,’ Sasha answered, ‘but that’s with a physio assessing your movement and strength, and they’ve all gone home already.’

Cam went closer still, caught sight through the door of an older woman hobbling as if her legs might give out at any moment.

‘Can we sign out against medical advice?’ someone asked.

Sasha replied, ‘The X-rays won’t be long. I’ll come back with the paperwork and the imaging, and then we’ll get you out of here.’ She stepped out into the hallway and then stopped. ‘Hi,’ she said, eyes wide, voice a murmur.

‘You need a physio?’ Cam offered.

‘Oh, ah, yeah.’ She looked as if she wanted to say something else. Instead, she glanced into the room, almost a shake of the head, then gave him a brief rundown of the case and introduced him to the Johansens.

And somehow, he held the idea, the one he’d been bursting to tell Sasha, somehow he kept it in his head. The consultation was quick: a standard checklist, a follow-up scheduled, and then the X-rays arrived and Sasha took over, discharging the happy couple with strict instructions not to pop it again getting in or out of the car—always a risk.

Sasha turned to Cam. ‘Can we talk?’

‘I figured it out.’ He was done waiting. ‘The body is the map, a three-dimensional complex terrain.’

She looked confused.

'Did you watch *The Magic School Bus* when you were a kid?' he asked.

'Ah, yeah, not every episode, but I've seen it.'

'The robotic assistant—it's like Ms Frizzle with GPS, guiding the surgeon's hands on the journey that is…the procedure.'

'Don't they always end up in strife?'

'Well, sure, but Ms Frizzle didn't have GPS.'

Sasha smiled. 'Everybody loves Ms Frizzle.'

'She's trustworthy, likeable, and always gets them home safe in the end.'

Sasha nodded and went silent.

'What?' he asked.

'I'm not likeable and trustworthy. I let you down. I'm surprised you still want to work on this at all after…yesterday.' She looked around the empty ward—they were alone, but no one was ever really alone on a ward—and started walking towards the break room.

'I do,' he said, pushing to catch up to her.

She stopped. 'But yesterday, you said—'

'I know. But I do trust you.'

She gave him a look as if she didn't know how to believe him, then marched ahead to the break room and held the door open so he could follow. Once it shut behind them, she stopped and faced him. He could see the fear in her eyes. Unshed tears, too.

'I was tired and angry,' he said. 'This whole funding thing, there are so many egos involved, hospital politics and big money, and I don't trust any of it, but I do trust you.'

She scoffed. 'Maybe you shouldn't. I just bowl on ahead, overconfident and blaming other people for the gaps when I'm the one—'

'You have an incredible mind and unique experience.'

'I'm overconfident. I think I know best.' She threw his own words back at him.

He reached out but she walked away. He wouldn't force it. But she had to know she wasn't the only one to blame here. 'I was so busy looking at your blind spot I forgot about my own.'

'And what's that?' She went to the kitchenette, poured a glass of water.

Jamming down the wheelchair brake, he got up and wedged the thing under the door handle—that'd do for a lock. This conversation was hard enough without surprise company. And, ideally, they wouldn't be overheard; he walked closer. There was still half a room between them and the distance ached, but crossing it felt impossible. 'How much did you overhear when you came out of surgery earlier?' he asked. 'In the observation room?'

'Enough.' She threw back her drink.

Shit, maybe he had made it worse. 'I couldn't just sit there and listen to them—'

She interrupted him. 'I don't want to know what they were saying.'

'You mean because you already know the exact sort of thing guys like that say about women who are smarter than them and have authority over them? Women who push back and make them better?'

'Make them better? I make them hate me. That doesn't make anything better.'

'That right there—how you manage to do what you need to do without burning it all down—that's my blind spot.'

She turned her back to him, leaning over the sink, splashing water on her face. 'I want to do better,' she said, dabbing a paper towel to her eyes. Shit, was she crying?

'I know.' Cam went over to her, the tightness in his legs an almost welcome discomfort—that kind of pain he knew exactly how to deal with, but this… Sasha was uncharted territory. He hadn't been here before—hadn't fallen in love, not like this.

Voice low, full of emotion, she went on, 'But you shouldn't have to…to teach me, to be responsible for my blind spots, my assumptions and questionable integrity.'

Cam felt that in his solar plexus. Damn straight, he shouldn't *have to*, but the mere fact of her saying it flipped a switch—he didn't have to, but he might choose to. Maybe he wanted to be that person for her, because, yeah, it would be nice for her to instinctively just *get it*, but no one could get that right all the time. And with Sasha, it would go both ways: she would do the same for him—shine a light on his blind spots, teach him things, keep him honest.

'I can't promise you it's all okay now,' she said.

'I really can't go and re-consent everyone on the application.'

'I know.'

'And this is a line in the sand for you, I get it. Your integrity is important and you don't have to keep working on the robotic-assistant thing.'

'The thing is…' he took her hand, pulled her to face him '… I want to—work with you. We're a good team.'

She nodded, tears spilling over onto her cheeks.

Sasha's heart was breaking. She could feel it happening, the ache opening up into a chasm. How was she supposed to keep working with him as if it didn't hurt just looking at him? All that they could have been was there between them, the weight of grief, of regret. He was holding her hand—she couldn't bear it and pulled away. 'We can finish what we started,' she said.

'Sasha, about last night, it wasn't just the funding and consents.'

'I know.' She didn't want him to say it. She already knew, and if he said it aloud, she'd have the words emblazoned in her memory, only making it worse. 'The HR thing,' she said, so he wouldn't. 'Don't worry about it. I got all caught up and rushed you. You're a nice guy and wanted to do the right thing.'

'What?'

'You don't have to say it.' *Please don't say it.*

'Sasha, you didn't rush me into anything. I fell for you, tumbled head over heels into this.'

'What?' She needed a moment to let that sink in, but he kept going:

'And as for the "nice guy" thing…' He swore. 'Yeah, I can get along with anyone and everyone, put on a smile, and be friendly, but I don't really let people in. A therapist would probably say it's self-protective, keeping people at arm's length. But you…you got past my defences. And I think, on some level, I was looking for a reason to kick you out, and set the bar impossibly high just to be sure no one could ever get close enough to hurt…'

She had hurt him—there it was. 'You deserve someone who can cross the high bar, Cam.'

'Not this bar. It's not for crossing. It's for making excuses because I'm scared. It's for sabotaging a good thing just in case it hurts.'

'I don't want to hurt you.' She reached out, wanting to touch him, but the space between them felt vast.

'I don't want to hurt you either, Sasha. But there's no point pretending—you want to be with me? You might not get to have the life you've imagined. There's no way of knowing what's coming. It won't always be smooth sailing.'

'I don't need smooth sailing.' She touched her fingertips to the centre of his chest—as much to reassure herself as him. She could reach him. This space between them wasn't impassable.

He covered her hand with his own. 'I hate the idea you'll miss out on anything because of me.'

'Missing out? Cam.' Sasha thought about the Johansens. Injuries and ageing, pain and uncertainty, those things were inevitable, but not having someone to lie down on the floor and hold hands with—that would be the real *missing out*.

'I have to be sure that you know what you're signing up for.'

She stepped closer, trapping their hands between their bodies. 'With you?'

He nodded, a look on his face as if it was entirely up to her, as if he was offering her everything, hers for the taking.

'I'm signing up for all of it.' She found her courage. 'I love you, Cam.'

There was a pause, a breath, and then his mouth crashed down on hers—nothing smooth and romantic about this kiss, only desperation and bruising relief. 'I love you,' he said on a breath between kisses, pulling her near, vanishing the last slip of distance between them.

Cam heard the words. On some level he knew she meant them. But he kissed her, at least in part, to keep her from saying it again. She loved him. She was signing up for all of it. Because she loved him.

It was so much—too much to take in.

So he kissed her instead, ran his hands around her body, held her tight, as if this was solid proof that she was real, and here, and in his arms, and he hadn't ruined everything—as if his senses could be so sure of her physical being that his mind would relent and her words would be real.

Her hands were on his face, her thumbs stroking his cheeks. He tasted salt in the kiss—her tears or his, no way of knowing. He broke away for air, but she only held him tighter, pressing her face into the crook of his neck, peppering kisses on his skin.

'Beaches are basically impossible,' he said. 'And if you want to hike the Abel Tasman, you'll have to go with someone else.'

She gave a breathy laugh and it slipped under his collar, lighting up every nerve raising goosebumps down his back.

'If you ever come to resent me…'

'I won't.'

'But if you do.'

She pulled away, just enough to look him in the eye. 'That older couple just now—when she fell, he told me he lay down on the floor beside her and held her hand while they waited for the ambulance.'

'That's what you want?'

'I want someone who'll stick with me even when I make mistakes, when I'm too much.'

'You're *not* too much.'

She cocked her head to the side, as if she didn't quite believe him, but as if she wanted to.

'You're *so* much—in the best way. More than I ever…' God, he was going to cry again if he finished that sentence—more than he'd dared to hope for. More than his heart could bear to lose. So instead, he said, 'I can pretty much guarantee I'll be the one falling over.'

'Give it long enough, I probably will too.'

Maybe his too-high bar wasn't too high after all. With those words, she cleared it. No more resisting; Cam let the soft heat of her mouth melt every other thought from his head.

EPILOGUE

FROM THE FRONT PORCH, Sasha could see snow on the mountains. She stepped out, barefoot, because it was so, so warm inside—Cam ran hot and, tucked up beside him, she was cosy as anything. Putting on slippers seemed unnecessary, and she had no idea where they were anyway, somewhere deep in the wardrobe, which had been overstuffed ever since she moved in, and they hadn't had time to sort it out. Work had been busy, and every minute they weren't working, there were better things to do than tidy the wardrobe.

So she stepped outside, braved the late-winter frost, and took the empty milk bottle out to the recycling on the kerb. She could hear the truck somewhere nearby, but not yet in sight—the tinkle of glass, the revving engine.

Her feet ached on the cold ground, and she would have rushed back inside, but then she saw it—a tiny white daffodil just peeking from the bud. The front lawn was white with frost, the gardens bare, plants dormant, as if spring was still a long, long way off. But now that she'd noticed the one early flower, she saw the other shoots, the tender green stems poking up out of the grass. In a day or two, there would be more—dozens of them.

She rushed inside. The wooden porch felt almost warm against her icy feet. 'Cam,' she called out, scuffing her soles against the *Nau mai haere mai* welcome mat. Come in, come close. It was more than just a welcome; it was *you belong now*.

'Did you beat the truck?' He came through from the kitchen in boxers and a hoodie, a triangle of toast in one hand, wheeling his chair with the other.

She nodded. 'There are daffodils already.'

'Oh, the erlicheer. Neroli got them at a school fair when Jules was…must have been five or six.'

Sasha followed him back into the kitchen, doing the maths—seven, maybe eight years ago now.

'I remember planting the bulbs with him,' Cam said. 'Neroli was annoyed because we dug up her lawn, but Mum said it was the best place for them. You forget they're there, and just when winter feels like it'll never end, up they pop.'

Sasha took her seat at the kitchen table. 'Erlicheer. Good name.'

'Your feet must be freezing,' Cam said, reaching for her legs.

Her toes tingled with the sudden warmth, tucked under his thigh.

He hissed and laughed. 'Good God, woman. Risking frostbite for a milk bottle.'

'Yeah, but I beat the truck.' She sipped her coffee. 'And the warmth is even better after the cold.'

Goodness, she sounded like an optimist—Cam really had rubbed off on her. Being with him, she didn't need to prepare for the worst, be on alert, ready for things to go wrong. Not because things wouldn't go wrong, but because they'd deal with it when it happened. Because she was sure of him, of *them*. And in the meantime, things could continue to go very, very right.

He reached down and kissed her knee, all he could reach. 'You sure you're warm enough?' he asked.

So she put down her coffee and scrambled over into his lap. 'I will be.'

* * * * *

If you enjoyed this story, check out this other great read from Amy Blythe

Emergency Room Reunion

Available now!